All characters and events within the story, other than those clearly in the public domain, are fictitious and any resemblance to real persons, living or dead, is purely coincidental

The Only One

A Dennison Property story

Acknowledgements

I'd like to take the opportunity to thank Debbie Ellis and Lucy my daughter, they were my sounding boards and the little voices that nagged at me to get done already. I'd also like to thank Vickie wood a talented acoustic guitarist, singer and songwriter who let me use her selfie to make the cover. Lastly I'd like to thank my other children, my 5 boys, who although at times they leave me exasperated, I wouldn't have it any other way. They are my reason to get up in the morning and I love them all more than I could ever say.

Chapter One

Kitty Phillips sighed as she finally stepped out of the lift into the work area she shared with Audrey Bennet, Blake Dennison's administrative assistant. She was tired, dishevelled, and immensely pleased to have arrived in one piece. Audrey appeared behind her out of the toilets.

'You're looking a little worse for wear?' she smiled sympathetically at her as she sat down at her desk.

'The bus turned up early and I had to run for it, in the rain', as she blew out a breath.

'I had to stand up all the way because it was packed, got coughed and sneezed on by a man who was obviously ill, then just for giggles, the driver let more people on' she said in disgust as she turned towards her own desk. She was just about to boot up her computer when raised voices came from behind Blake's office door, she raised a querying brow at Audrey who just shrugged her shoulders.

****

Blake had been scrutinizing details on his latest deal when Natalia Jenson stormed unannounced into his office. The Icelandic blonde, paced around shouting in both Swedish and English, her arms waving around like a windmill as she gesticulated wildly.

He looked on in stunned disbelief when it suddenly went quiet, so quiet his ears were ringing as she sucked in air and opened her mouth to start again. Snapped out of his dazed stupor Blake pushed his chair back angrily as he stood up and slammed his hands down on his desk, gaining her stunned attention.

'Out!' he shouted at her furiously, his own anger roused with his indignation. He didn't have a clue who she thought she was?

Coming into his office without an invitation and making a spectacle of them both, he was absolutely livid.

He hadn't laid eyes on her since he'd stupidly taken her to a fundraising event and not taken her up on the obvious invitation afterwards. He was bored, even the sex had lost its appeal. An unsatisfying release with interchangeable, unchallenging but beautiful women. They'd all began to blur together, none of them especially memorable, or appealing, where was the challenge? He needed something more, someone to stimulate his brain and body and sighed at the whole sorry mess.

'But……..' she started to wheedle, rolling her rounded hips in an exaggerated fashion, with her hands held out before her imploringly, as she slowing made her way over to him.

'No, I don't want to hear it' he told her through clenched teeth; as she again tried to speak. 'I thought you'd have gotten the message when I dropped you off and didn't call again'.

She didn't move, just looked at him, blinking in bewilderment as if she couldn't understand and he sighed wearily

'Just leave, we're through, I'm sorry, but we're over' her bottom lip wobbled and he tutted impatiently, fed up with the theatrics he gestured with his head towards his door. When she still didn't move his patience ran out completely, he stomped past her and yanked open the door himself and motioned for her to leave.

****

In the outer office, Kitty turned back to Audrey in query when his office door was snatched open, making them both jump as it hit the wall. There holding it open stood a stony-faced Blake, all 6 foot 3 inches of him. He was positively vibrating with anger, his jaw locked, a tick beginning in his cheek. He did the tall dark, brooding and gorgeous male to perfection.

Kitty froze in shock at her thoughts, where the hell had that come from? But then it turned to annoyance as her heart sped up like a freight train in her chest as she stood blankly staring at him. She was confused by her reaction and was unsure how to handle it, what to do, think, or even how to react as a stunning Blonde brushed passed him. She turned away, blanking out the scene, both internally and with Blake, until he spoke.

'Kitty please escort Miss Jenson down to the lobby and make sure security has her removed from the premises will you!' With that he turned on his heel and slammed his door shut in the face of the three speechless women; the loud bang reverberated around the silent office.

Kitty walked slowly towards the woman, running her hand nervously down her skirt as she cleared her throat.

'This way please, Miss Jenson' she said as she lead the way towards the lift and let out a relieved breath as she quietly followed her in. She'd been expecting a scene but it seemed the woman had deflated somewhat. She leaned negligently against the elevator wall, arms crossed as she tapped the toe of one of her excessively high heels impatiently, while she watched the floor's count down.

Ted from security stepped forward as the lift doors opened and gestured with his arm towards the revolving door, she flounced past him and swept out of the building in a cloud of indignation and heavy perfume.

Kitty rolled her eyes and gave Ted a strained smile as the lift doors closed on her again, leaving her alone with her thoughts. She had a few appointments to clarify with Blake and a mid-morning meeting to sort out. She blew out a breath as she caught sight of her reflection in the floor length chromed mirror and tutted, several strands of her hair had escaped confinement. She undid a couple of pins and re-twisted her hair with her hands to put it back into tidy order. She'd just slipped the last pin back in place as the doors opened again on her floor and stepped out.

Kitty walked to her own desk and dropped wearily into her seat putting her coat behind her, over the back of her chair and blew out a weary breath. Audrey made sympathetic noises from her own desk.

'Well that was a good start to the day' she said grumpily.

Audrey burst out laughing as she looked at her computer screen. Kitty shook her head in bewilderment, the woman found something funny in most situations, it was damn near impossible to ruffle her feathers. She had a backbone of steel, a good heart, and a quick mind and Kitty was extremely fond of her.

She wiggled her toes under her table and grimaced as she removed one of the new flat shoes she'd purchased for work. They looked nicer than they felt and mentally promised her feet a good soaking when she got home to make up for the abuse they'd received. As she slipped her foot back in she caught sight of Audrey out of the corner of her eye at the kettle doctoring two coffees. She placed one down near Kitty's hand, then went back to her own desk, dropped back into her chair and sighed with pleasure as she took a fortifying sip of the warm aromatic drink.

'Now that's why I'm an Administrative Assistant and not a P A. Type, file, field a few calls and not have to handle the aftermath of his little affairs'. She winked at Kitty's startled expression and laughed openly with derision before sobering and taking another sip.

'One day, you'll learn to let it all sail over your head' she said sympathetically, then put down her cup and continued with her work, a smile playing on her lips.

Blake wasn't bad to work for, kitty thought, he wasn't abusive or overly friendly; which was a definite bonus: she'd been around a few of those over her 27 years. On the down side, the man was handsome as sin and had women falling over themselves to get into his bed. Unfortunately, part of her job was fielding his calls and deciding whom to, or not to put through, depending on whom was flavour of the month, she thought disgustedly.

Then there came the job of purchasing the "kiss off gift", once the affair ended; which of course they always did. She then realised that that hadn't happened in the last couple of months. Oh, the calls still came in with nauseating regularity, but he hadn't requested any purchases to be bought or sent in a while. Not that she was interested in his sex life, she really wasn't. She had a new relationship of her own now, the first one she'd had in 2 years.

A few weeks ago she'd attended a fundraiser for spinal damage research, Audrey's husband headed the charity after he'd been involved in a car accident several years ago, leaving him in a wheelchair. She'd spent most of the evening trying not to stare in sick fascination as Blake's date had tried to keep her breasts from falling out of her too low, too short and too tight dress. Funnily enough, the very woman he'd just thrown out of the building.

Lance Edmonton was witty, articulate and although as handsome as Blake, his looks were more subtle, not as masculine. His physique was more on the lines or a runner where Blake was built along body builder proportions, wide shoulders and thick arms but they both had height. He had stopped her on her way back from the toilets and struck up a conversation. He'd then pursued her persistently and flatteringly for over a fortnight before she'd finally agreed to a date; much to Blake's annoyance. He had tried talking her out of it, apparently there was some "bad blood" between them, not that that had anything to do with her. Blake was concerned for her, due to Lance reputation. "Kettle and pot" she'd thought at the time but had kept that to her-self as she'd thanked him politely for his concern. Not that she needed or wanted it, she was old enough to make her own decisions. After 2 years of celibacy she was finally ready to dip her toe in the dating pool.

She'd never had a vexed woman in the office before though, that was a new one and exceedingly embarrassing to boot. He normally kept them out of his workspace, not that they ever seemed to last very long. She didn't know what his problem was, the ones she'd spoken to seemed personable enough. They were usually blonde and beautiful, well the ones she'd seen pictures of him with in magazines at various functions. Not so much the earlier one though, she'd looked down her nose at Audrey and herself at the Spinal damage fundraiser.

The only reason she could think of for the way Blake changed women was that he was a bit of a player, the same as her brother and he had commitment issues, men like him usually did; her brother sure did: much to their father's annoyance.

****

Blake sat down tiredly to gather himself before continuing his work schedule, he was still furious that the woman had dared to come badgering him at his office. He groaned when he thought about the unprofessional scene that his employees had been witness to, especially Kitty. He was usually much better at distancing his personal life but he was a little preoccupied at the moment.

His sister was off to a specialist neonatal unit in Birmingham later in the day for a risky procedure to try to save the lives of her unborn twins and he was worried for her and them both.

She was married to his head accountant and one of his closest friends, Mike Berkley. Blake, Len Simpson, head of his Legal team and Mike had met at University when they'd all been naïve 18 year olds. Mike was a walking calculator, with a sharp business mind but the thing Blake liked best about him these days was that he adored his wife Melanie, Blake's sister.

He had a meeting planned for this afternoon, and he and Mike needed had to discuss the feasibility of him acquiring a failing hotel, before he left shortly. He wanted to add it to his portfolio, but he'd have to see what problems it was having first. What he didn't need was distractions, he needed his wits about him but the biggest distraction at the moment was his sex life or lack thereof, he'd always used sex as a stress reliever, so going without wasn't helping. He knew the lack was his own fault, but tension due to sexual frustrated on top of everything else he had going on at the moment, he could do without.

Maybe he needed to rectify that and quickly, lower his expectations but damn it no one appealed at the moment and sighed in frustration as he ran his fingers through his hair. No time for self-pity today, he needed to get his head in the game, he'd worry about rectifying that particular problem after the meetings.

'Kitty can you come through please' came Blake's disembodied voice through the intercom.

She finished her coffee in two swallows, without burning her tongue and picked up her note pad and diary, walking to his door, she blew out a breath, knocked and entered.

He sat behind his desk perusing something on his computer and motioned her to sit down all without taking his eyes off the screen. He tapped a pen distractedly against his desk while he visualised what he needed to get done short-term.

'Okay, contact Jake Masterson and put off the meeting until 1.30pm, I need to speak to Mike about a couple of things before he leaves for Birmingham' he then lifted his eyes from the screen. 'I'd also appreciate you taking an early lunch as I need you to sit in on the meeting' he looked towards her and she nodded her consent. 'Good' he smiled at her 'that'll be all for now Kitty, I think you have enough to be going on with until then' and his attention once again went back to his screen as she got up and left the room, leaving a subtle but sultry scent behind her. He drew in an appreciative breath before frowning at his behaviour. "Since when did he notice how Kitty smelt?"

Letting the disturbing thought go, Blake gave Mike a quick ring to make sure he was on his way up with the revised figures he had available to him, he needed to see them before he made any major moves.

Kitty made the requested calls, pulled the files required for the meeting and got on with the preparation for this afternoons meeting, as Audrey carried on with her own work. She dealt with external correspondence between Blake and the various departments and contractors they used outside of the building.

Mike had been and gone, she'd wished him luck as he'd left. She'd then put a couple of query calls through to Blake and was shocked to find the morning had gone as she spotted the time. She closed down her computer, arranged the files she needed for when she got back and pulled on her coat.

'I'm off to meet Lance for lunch,' she informed Audrey

'I didn't know you had a lunch date today?'

'Neither does he, I'm going to surprise him' Kitty grinned as the doors closed on Audrey's laugh.

A 5 minute stroll had her in front of the building Lance rented floor space in, she acknowledge the receptionist at the main desk as she passed by on her way to the lift.

There was no Assistant sat at the desk outside his office, she saw as she stepped out of the lift onto his floor and walked towards his door.

Rapping lightly, she pushed it open and came to a standstill, frozen in the doorway, her mouth open in surprise at the sight that greeted her. Her shock turned to disbelief as she spun angrily on her heel and walked away, leaving the door open in her haste to escape.

She stormed angrily back across the floor to the lift, jabbed the button and stepped inside as the doors opened for her and hit the ground floor button aggressively. Just as the doors started to close on her, Lance appeared out of his office, his blonde hair mussed up, hastily fastening his pants. His slate grey eyes turned stormy with displeasure as he took in her mulish stance and defiant middle finger salute; just as the lift doors closed.

She walked out of the lift in a daze, she couldn't believe what she'd walked in on. She left the building, half-heartedly waving goodbye to the smiling receptionist, and made the short journey back to work on autopilot.

****

Audrey was on her lunch and Blake was just leaving his office to grab a sandwich as Kitty walked silently back out of the lift and dropped down into her chair at her desk, oblivious to him and her surroundings as he stopped at her side. Her expression was totally blank.

'Oh Kitty you're back, Audrey said you were having lunch with Lance?' She looked up at him in surprise as she hung her coat back over her chair behind her

'He was otherwise ………… engaged with his

Assistant,' she told him scathingly, as her lashes lowered, covering her eyes.

'Okay' he said, mystified by her strange mood 'are you meeting him later?' not that he was interested, he detested Edmonton, he was just trying to figure out what was wrong with her. She snorted as she tapped her short manicured nail against her chin, staring off into space, seemingly deep in thought, while he waited, his concern growing.

'Erm let me think …….. nope' she popped the p, 'I don't think I'll be seeing him, ever again' she said as she leaned sideways and looked down at her legs, seemingly engrossed with something she'd spotted. He was flummoxed, her behaviour was completely out of character, she was usually polite, not one for gossip or sarcasm and always annoyingly self-contained. He'd often told her she needed to speak up if she had a problem.

He cleared his throat, unsure what to say but uncomfortable with her whole demeanour, when without lifting her head and in a decidedly flat voice, said.

'Do you know, the term Personal Assistant took on a whole new connotation this afternoon'. Then went silent before continuing. 'I never realised giving the boss head was part of the job description? .... go figure huh. Guess I missed that class'. And on that bomb shell she gracefully stood from her desk, grabbed her bag off the floor and walked away.

He stood open mouthed, staring at her retreating back, speechless for the first time in his life. It wasn't what she'd said, not really, it was that she'd said it so matter of fact.

She stopped as she neared the toilets and turned, pinning him with spitting green eyes

'What is it with guys like you? You seem to think that women are there for your own personal sexual gratification. If we don't deliver, you move on to the next available prospect. You all make me sick' she spat, turned and banged her hand against the toilet door to open it. It snapped shut behind her as he stood rooted to the spot, open mouthed, staring at the closed door.

He stood immobile, too stunned to move, she'd just insulted him, and it royally pissed him off, his temper thawing his shock. He stormed after her and slammed through the door too, coming to a halt as the door slid from his lax grip and clicked shut.

She had her right shoe off and her leg on a chair as she rolled down a black stocking as she looked at him over her shoulder, her black brow rose in silent query as she continued with her task while she waited for him to speak.

'What the bloody hell was that about?' he shouted, his eyes sweeping hungrily over the length of naked leg and thigh on display.

She stooped to grab a new stocking out of her bag and slid it up her leg as he watched in rapt fascination. She dropped her foot, slipped it back into her shoe and smoothed down her skirt as she tossed the other stocking in the bin, then turned and glared at him.

'Have you seen enough?' she snarled, as warm colour crept up his face. He hadn't meant to stare, I mean he'd never looked at her before, not really looked, he usually avoided it. She was his P A for god sake, damned good at her job, and out of bounds. He cleared his throat in discomfort and squirmed at the realisation of being caught ogling her like he was hungry and she was steak.

'I apologise,' he said, shamefaced. 'I didn't think before I followed you in here' he gestured around them, feeling wrong footed before remembering why he'd followed her in the first place and his annoyance re-surfaced as he thundered', you insulted me, and I'd like to know why?'

She snorted, hands on her hips, the action opening her jacket and bringing her small waist and ample breasts to his attention.

'Oh please, you and Lance are one and the same' she sneered and took a shuddering breath before continuing 'You know you're good looking men and use it shamelessly to treat women like dispensable play things' she raked her eyes over him with disgust. 'Dumb, blow up dolls who's only purpose is to temporarily service your sexual whims before you move on to your next conquest' she spat at him throwing her arms up in the air in anger 'you both make me sick the way you go through women like bloody shirts' she said as he stared at her in rapt fascination.

'You once told me to speak up, so here goes, I'm sick of dealing with the women that come and go through that revolving door in your bedroom and I'm handing in my notice, deal with your own bloody mess from now on'.

She pushed passed him, shoulder checking him on her way out of the toilets, leaving him again standing there open mouthed, but this time he was simmering with rage.

She stomped back to her desk and turned on her computer to type up her resignation, hitting the keys more forcefully than necessary but she was livid. She needed to hit something desperately and better her keyboard than her boss, or soon to be "ex-boss", she thought.

2 years she'd worked for him and in that time she'd lost count of how many personal calls she'd fielded for him, she couldn't stomach the thought of doing it any more. She pictured his ex-lover storming out of the office this morning and how superior she'd felt, thinking she was immune to such things and snorted at her own naivety by yet again being taken for a fool by a player.

She'd thought they were going somewhere. She knew from the start that his reputation was as bad as Blake's but had stupidly thought he saw her differently after the way he'd pursued her. "I'm obviously delusional" she hissed under her breath. She couldn't believe she'd fallen for the lines again, she should have gone with her original instincts and steered clear. She'd let the loneliness of the last couple of years get to her, had decided that maybe it was time to try again, she'd spent enough time licking her wounds after the last one. How many times could one person get it so wrong?

A memory stirred of a conversation she'd had with Blake concerning Lance and her anger fizzed out as she realised what she'd just done. She bit her lip in uncertainty as she heard the toilet door open behind her and slam forcefully against the wall. She winced as she was pulled bodily out of her chair by her arm and hauled un-ceremonially out of the outer office and into Blake's. The door slammed and locked behind them as he pulled her around to face him.

He towered over her, his chest heaving as his dark chocolate brown eyes zeroed in on her face, then her mouth, she could feel the sexual tension crackling in the air and knowing what was coming next had her panicked.

She took a step back her heart slamming in her chest as he stared hungrily at her, his top lip flattening and making his bottom one appear fuller. A nerve ticked at the side of his jaw, his eyebrows had become a dark slash of colour in his handsome angry face and her mouth dried as he took a step closer. She tried to move backwards but her nervous flight was stopped abruptly, as her bottom hit his desk and she came to a standstill.

He walked slowly towards her as she stood trapped against his desk, he was absolutely incensed with the verbal attack he'd just received, without provocation. He was absolutely furious that she'd compared him to bloody Edmonton, him, how dare she. Edmonton's reputation with women was appalling; he'd warned her about him himself for god sake. He was nothing like him. He treated his partners with respect, well usually, not counting this morning's episode and inwardly winced at the memory.

He wasn't a "wham, bam, thank you mam" kind of man, not that he was an angel, far from it but he was nothing like him and not just where women were concerned either. He tried desperately to reign in his temper before he said or did something he'd later regret. He focused on his breathing as he watched her, and she watched him warily in return.

The longer he watched the more he noticed little things about her that he'd never picked up on before, like the loose suit's she favoured that hid her curvaceous figure. The skirts ending well below her knees, perfectly respectable, designed to hide the long shapely legs he'd just feasted his eyes on.

Her raven Black hair was always pulled back unappealingly into that god awful twist at the back of her head, but it still managed to emphasise her high cheek bones. Her arched brows and long black lashes emphasised her green slanted eyes, which now he was really looking at them realised they were spectacular. They had an outer ring of gold and specks of brown, he became transfixed as they darkened from emerald to jade, her pupils dilating, only leaving a very slim ring of gold. He couldn't decide if it was because she was attracted to, or scared of him, so he took an experimental step towards her.

A cruelly satisfied smile broke over his face as her berry tinted lips parted and warm colour suffused her usually clear, honey smooth complexion. He heard her breath catch in her throat and watched in rapt fascination as her breasts rose and fell in her agitation, the action thrusting them against one of the white blouses she favoured. She always had them buttoned up to her neck, no hint of cleavage on show; Kitty wasn't the flirty type, but they did showcase her slender neck.

He was astounded that he'd never noticed all these little details about her before, not that he was blind, he assured himself, it was just that he liked to keep a certain amount of distance and professionalism between himself and his staff. It was just so startling to see, the woman before him was a changeling, and she'd been hiding in plain sight all this time.

He mentally replayed the words she'd thrown at him and nearly laughed out loud. She genuinely believed he was no better than Edmonton, now that was damn insulting in itself, but that he had a revolving bedroom door. Well maybe in his youth he conceded, he had thrown himself into the dating scene back then, gorging himself on all that was freely offered but as time had worn on the thrill had diminished. Women had become less of a challenge and he'd lost interest in the whole thing the last year or so but he wasn't disinterested now, far from it, Kitty had his full, undivided attention.

His smile became wider, friendlier, showing off his straight white teeth as he watched her pink tongue slip out and run over her bottom lip nervously before her teeth bit into it. He watched as it was released and plumped back up, leaving it damp and fuller. He nearly groaned as he thought of leaning forward and tasting her, he took another experimental step towards her, his chest stopping scant inches from hers, so close he could feel the heat rising off her body and caught that elusive scent that she used. It was a subtle, pleasant spice that teased his nostrils and above that he could just make out the scent of the lemon shampoo she used, together the mix was evocative, sensual.

He took a deep breath, drawing it deep into his lungs, his nostrils flaring at the tantalising aroma and had to clench his hands at his sides to stop himself from reaching for her. "She really thought she had him pegged did she? Well she was in for one hell of a surprise", he thought with deep satisfaction, as his eyes swept over her possessively.

He usually didn't mix business with pleasure but as she was threatening to resign, she'd just removed any barriers on that score as far as he was concerned. She'd thrown down the gauntlet and he was more than happy to pick it up. For the first time in a very long while he was anticipating the chase. He was a predator at heart, that's why his business did so well, he could smell weakness and knew when to strike and how to succeed. Kitty had just become his latest target.

He sidestepped her, needing space between them to alleviate some of the tension riding his libido. He was definitely calmer now he had a plan and moved around his desk and sat down silently.

'Sit down Kitty, we have things to discuss' he informed her and watched as she swivelled warily to look at him, before carefully lowering herself into the chair opposite him.

She sucked in a steadying breath as he put space between them, her heart rate beginning to slow. She'd never been more aware of her own sexuality than when his body heat had begun to seep into her own oversensitive skin.

His scent had enveloped her, a natural warm musk, with a citrus undertone that had teased her nostrils and made her nipples tighten painfully. She'd always avoided looking directly at him, had known instinctively that he could be dangerous to her and now knew she'd been "dead on the money", and her pulse sped up again at the thought.

Now she'd finally given herself permission to look, she couldn't seem to tear her eyes away from him. She greedily catalogued his astounding features from under her lashes. She was use to good looking men, her dad and brother were amazingly handsome men but there was a dangerous raw quality to Blake's looks that they didn't possess. Blake's sex appeal scared her on a fundamental level.

His intelligent eyes weren't just dark chocolate, they had a lighter ring of topaz around the pupil with amber flecks in the iris. His lashes were so thick and dark they'd have looked feminine on any other man. His brows were thick but nicely shaped and only emphasised his broad forehead and sharp cheekbones. He had a straight full nose and a chiselled jaw that seemed to have a permanent five o'clock shadow and his mouth, oh god his mouth was glorious. His bottom lip was fuller and he was built for raw pleasure and she shuddered at the thought of what his mouth was capable of.

His naturally tousled hair was not only dark brown but had natural streaks of gold and blonde highlights running through it, it shone with health as it swept lovingly over his forehead. It was long enough to touch his collar, and her hands had itched to brush it back over his ears as he'd stared her down. His powerfully built frame had left her feeling feminine and dainty as he'd towered over her 5 feet 7, and had been frankly horrified a how spectacularly she'd underestimated his appeal to her. She'd felt confused and betrayed by how wantonly her body's response had been to his proximity.

She sat quietly waiting for him to speak, her bravado had long ago faded leaving her feeling foolish and drained after her earlier outburst. She tore her eyes away from his too intelligent gaze as he sat silently observing her, like an intriguing specimen under a microscope and she swallowed nervously.

His long fingers were a steeple under his chin, elbows resting on his desk, giving a deceptively relaxed pose. He silently watched her squirm in remorse, the heightened colour of her temper fading from her face, leaching her of colour. Gone was the magnificent heightened vibrancy of earlier, leaving her looking tired and vulnerable and his gut clenched in sympathy. He ruthlessly stamped down on it, now was not the time to show weakness and back down, too much was at stake, his peace of mind for one, plus he was going to have her, he would accept no other outcome.

'I know you're angry and from what I've surmised from your outburst, I believe rightly so. But you're taking it out on the wrong man' he informed her succinctly. He leaned forward and he held up his hand to silence the protest he knew was coming. 'Your ex?' he raised his brow and waited patiently for confirmation and smiled with satisfaction as she lowered her gaze from him and nodded her agreement to his statement. 'Edmonton' he spat the word contemptuously, 'has behaved abominably and while I can sympathise, I am not him and I don't appreciate the comparison'.

He took a breath and leaned back into his chair, trying to making himself less threatening now he'd made his point.

'If you really want to leave my employment?, I won't be happy but I won't stop you, but may I just suggest you think very carefully about it before you make any hasty decisions' he added. He phrased it to make it appear as if it was of no consequence to him one way or the other, when in theory it mattered immensely. He'd planted the idea of her staying. He enjoyed this particular part of the game he was a master at subtle manipulation and he squelched the guilt that tried to rise.

'I have never requested anything of you that isn't the normal undertaking of a Personal Assistant, after all it is your job to make sure my life runs smoothly'. He sat quietly then giving her time to digest his words, while he planned his next move, he had plenty of time, he was confident that she wasn't going anywhere. Not in the short-term anyway.

He could be patient when he wanted something badly enough and now he knew she had claws, he most definitely wanted Kitty.

He just had to decide how and when? and allowed himself a moment to savour the thought.

Chapter two

Kitty sat quietly taking notes at the meeting between Blake and Jake Masterson. She was still rather subdued after her earlier blow out, she'd thought she had her temper under control but it seemed to have slipped the leash there for a while.

Blake watched her from the corner of his eye as she sat quietly, her fabulous legs crossed and her head bent as she studiously took notes. She was turning out to be an enigma and he was beginning to be slightly concerned, he seemed to be paying more attention to working her out than he was on Jake Masterson.

He listened only half attentively as Jake lay out all the problems that had affected the hotel, turning a thriving business into a losing prospect. Suddenly Kitty raised her head, brow furrowed.

'I'm sorry Mr Masterson, but can you repeat that last part please,?' she requested and he sighed dejectedly as he relayed the problems of the increased interest payments he'd had to find for his backer due to a clause he'd not noticed in the contract he'd taken out with him. The constant delays of provisions and substandard food deliveries that had been received, that had then had to be replaced so as not to affect the restaurants reputation. He'd lost a chef, poached for another less upmarket establishment for a higher salary. He explained that his backer was getting nasty, badgering him to sign over the hotel. Another clause he hadn't been aware of, giving the backer the right to take his business from him if he fell behind with the payments, thus meaning the backer could sell on the business and re-coup his losses. If it went that way he'd lose everything, not just his time and money but also his reputation in the business. He'd lose everything in one fell swoop, with no recompense and no home.

Kitty eyes met Blake's for the first time since walking back through his door and he saw the intelligence and interest sparkling there.

He knew she was thinking along the same lines as him, that his backer was out for blood and was probably sabotaging the business to get his hands on it.

Blake cleared his throat

'It seems clear from the earlier figures that the business was doing exceeding well originally, regular re-bookings and a good standard of food?' Jake nodded. 'Well give me a couple of days to check through all the details' Blake added 'I'll also get my legal department to go through your backers contract with a fine tooth comb' he said. 'If everything goes the way I hope it does, I may be able to help you' he said and Jake Masterson sat up straighter, losing some of the hopelessness and despair that had clung to him since he'd entered the office.

Kitty didn't look up as Blake made this announcement, though she had to admit to being a little surprised. Most people in his position would have left the seller in the dark to make the most profit, after all that's what big business came down to. He had just gone up in

her estimation but she refused to meet his eyes. She could feel him watching her as she pretended to be engrossed in her work.

'Jake, just give me a couple of days to go through some facts and figures and I'll get back to you'. Jake stood up and looked indecisive, his slight build seeming to shrink more in his agitation.

'I give you my word, we'll sort this out for you, one way or another' Blake said as he got up from his desk to walk him to the door.

Kitty got up and started pulling all the paperwork together, her mind going over the problem's as Blake closed the door and stood leaning back against it. He wanted to just spend a few moments alone with her to see if he could make her drop her guard and relax around him. It wouldn't do his plans any good if he couldn't get her to trust him, he needed to get to know the real Kitty, the woman behind the mask. He was ashamed to admit that he knew very little about her. He didn't know if she had any living family, her interests, her taste in food, music and literature and he definitely wanted to get close to her. Intimately close.

Kitty felt her pulse start to accelerate as he leaned against the closed door, his arms crossed over his broad chest, pulling on his shirt; showcasing his amazing physique as he watched her silently. She felt like a bug under a microscope, his eyes held hers as he slowly uncrossed his arms and moved slowly towards her. He stopped just in front of her and her heart beat out a rapid tattoo in her chest, her stomach fluttered and her mouth dried. She was in trouble here, he had an instantaneous effect on her now and all it had taken was a look. She was disgusted with her traitorous body, she cleared her throat to try and shift the feeling of constriction she felt there.

He could see the pulse in her neck beating double time as he closed in on her and although he'd like nothing better than to taste it, he knew that rushing would be a mistake. She'd slap a harassment suit on him and be gone so fast she'd leave skid marks on the floor. This was going to take some finesse on his part, he hadn't had to rely on that for a long time and was a little disconcerted to find that he was a little rusty in that area, especially where she was concerned. He hadn't wanted anyone this bad in a long time, if ever?

'Kitty are we good?' he asked as he lowered his eyes and moved back around his desk, taking his seat again. She nodded but didn't speak.

'Good, sit down I want to use you as a sounding board' he said and waited while she took the seat in front of his desk. Maybe if he included her in this project, it would help break the ice and hopefully end the air of tension between them.

Kitty sat back down again and tried to relax but her earlier outburst was still playing on her mind.

'I'm really sorry about earlier Blake, I had no right to say the things I did' she informed him, as she chanced a look at him, he was looking directly at her and his eyes trapped and held hers as he gave her a warm, friendly smile.

'Let's just forget it ever happened and carry on as before shall we?' he said the tension easing in his chest when she nodded her agreement. He back in his seat and took a relieved breath, she didn't trust him yet, but it was a start.

'Okay Kitty, what are your feelings on this deal?' he said watching her eyes widen and her mouth part in shock as she stared at him. He realised that in all the time she'd worked for him, he'd never once asked her opinion about a specific deal and could have kicked himself. Maybe some subconscious part of him had been aware of the possibility for attraction between them from the beginning and that's why he hadn't used her as a sounding board as he would have usually done with his P A.

Kitty cleared her throat and thought over the problems that the hotel had been having, cataloguing the errors and flicked through the report on her knee.

'Well it seems to me that someone wants the business to fail'. He nodded as she continued. 'I think it would be prudent to look into the food orders first, figure out if there is one particular person who's doing the ordering or if there's more than one, then I'd look at the suppliers themselves. If I'd have been him though, I'd have taken over that particular job myself, well short term anyway until I'd gotten to the bottom of the problems'. She started to warm to the subject, after all this was an area she'd grown up in. 'I'd also check out the kitchen staff to make sure the problem isn't centred there'. She took a deep breath 'If you want my honest opinion, I'd have a complete overhaul of staff and training, check into their backgrounds and try to nip the problem in the bud. If the staff aren't loyal they need to go, that would ensure this kind of problem doesn't arise again'.

He was smiling openly at her now, the warmth reaching his eyes, turning them into pools of warm milk chocolate, shot through with flecks of caramel, and her stomach turned over.

'Well it seems we're on the same page, how do you fancy eating out this evening?' He knew the change of topic had thrown her, but he didn't want her to think too hard. He could see the refusal forming so rushed on. 'I think it would be a good idea to book a table at the hotel restaurant while it's still open, get a feel for the place. I find I get a more realistic view when I approach these things from a customer's point of view, rather than management or owner' he added 'I did the same with the gyms I bought, spent time there as a client to get a feel for the place before I made any decisions'.

Kitty could understand where he was coming from, she knew it made good business sense but she wasn't sure spending time out of the office with him was a good idea. She knew she was attracted to him and that spending time alone with him over a candle lit meal was asking for trouble. She should refuse but if she did she'd have to give him a reason and as she'd just ended a relationship she couldn't use a previous commitment. She was going to have to bite the bullet here and just deal with it, I mean how hard could it be to spend a couple of hours alone with him and groaned in her head. This had disaster written all over it.

'I think it would be a good idea' she heard herself agreeing and hoped to god she didn't live to regret it.

'Excellent I'll pick you up at eight, I'll book the table for around eight forty five' he responded not giving her a chance to make up an excuse.

'We'll talk more over the meal' he informed her as he turned back to his computer screen, supposedly engrossed in the information there. Dismissed, she reluctantly got up from her chair. He knew she wasn't happy, he'd watched from the corner of his eye as her shoulders had drooped in defeat. He refused to feel guilty, he was going to use every dirty trick in the book to get what he wanted, and he wanted her.

He smiled to himself as his door closed behind her and picked the phone up to make the reservation himself, humming gleefully as he managed to arrange a table in a secluded spot. It was all falling into place, now all he had to do was tread carefully, try not to do anything that would throw up her defences and grinned in anticipation. He would just lay on the charm, be witty and attentive, I mean how hard could it possibly be? She was just a woman and they seemed to like him well enough.

Kitty returned gloomily to her desk, opened up a new document and started to type up the notes she'd just taken, including her thoughts on areas to be looked into.

'Hey, why the long face?' Audrey queried

'No reason, just a business dinner with Blake, tonight' she replied stiltedly then froze as she heard Audrey whistle appreciatively.

'Well honey, if I was a few years younger, foot loose and fancy free, I'd be doing a jig at the thought of having that fine man to myself for an evening' she informed her with a saucy wink

'It's a business dinner, he just wants to get a feel for the hotel he's thinking of purchasing' Kitty replied hastily before she got the wrong idea.

'Well if I was in your shoes, I'd be thinking about getting a feel of him' she quipped, without missing a beat, oblivious to Kitty's discomfort as she squirmed in her seat as she still had her own eyes on her screen.

'It'll do you good, get out and live a little, enjoy yourself, get back on the bike, so to speak'.

'I'm not riding Blake' Kitty squeaked in horror, then nearly bit her tongue off as she realised what she'd just said. She groaned aloud at the dirty laugh that came from Audrey.

'Honey if I was you, I'd ride that man like a pony' she deadpanned and Kitty couldn't help it, she burst out laughing, feeling her subdued mood lift with the light hearted banter. For the first time since the sorry mess with Lance earlier, she felt more like herself.

'You are incorrigible' she scolded Audrey with a shake of her head, as she continued typing up her own notes. She was feeling more optimistic after Audrey's ribbing, she could do this, have a nice platonic evening out with her boss. After all there was no way he was interested in her, she wasn't his type, he dated blondes and that she definitely was not.

He also kept his work and personal life separate, well normally, the earlier mess was not the normal way he operated, so everything would be fine, she assured herself. They'd get a feel for the place, sample the food and atmosphere and end the evening without a problem. All she had to do was keep a friendly but professional head on and everything would be fine.

She could cope? She hoped.

Chapter Three

Blake pulled up outside Kitty's home just before 8pm, switched off his sat nav and took an interested look around the neighbourhood. It was quiet but nice, neat gardens, not highly prosperous but there again he'd been brought up on a much rougher council estate he mused. He got out of the car, clicked the key fob to lock it and walked up the short path. She lived in the ground floor flat of the converted, two storied Victorian house and he could see lights coming from several windows. He knocked and waited for her to answer, his interest piqued as he heard the tap of heels, "ooh that's new" he'd never known her wear anything but flats in all the time she'd worked for him.

Kitty had been undecided on what to wear; she didn't want to give the wrong impression as this wasn't a date but business over a meal. She wanted to give of a casual but professional air and pulled several outfits out before she'd finally settled on one. She'd taken too long she realised as she took a horrified look at the bedside clock, he would be arriving in 20 minutes. She would have preferred to meet him there but as the hotel wasn't on a bus route and she didn't own a car; her own stubbornness as she refused to take charity from her parents. She'd had to concede defeat on him collecting her, she wasn't flush enough to order taxi's everywhere; even though she probably could have put the fare price down as a business expense.

She'd showered in record time, dried her long hair and pulled on clean underwear. She threw on a Jade green blouse, a lightweight pair of black trousers and added a pair of small heels, to make her feel less vulnerable by his height. She'd just dabbed on her favourite evening scent and a touch of mascara and tinted lip gloss when she heard the knocking. She rushed down the hallway flustered and pulled opened the door.

Blake nearly swallowed his tongue as she appeared at the door looking flustered and absolutely stunning without her glasses.

Some kind of recognition flickered in his subconscious but didn't come to full fruition, before disappearing again.

'Come in, I won't be a moment' she told him as she turned and moved back down the hallway at a clip, disappearing behind a door to his right. He shook himself, stunned by the view of her jet black hair swishing down her back with every step, it stopped just short of her rounded bottom. He hadn't even noticed what she'd been wearing as his whole attention had been riveted on that moving fall of black silk.

He had visions of wrapping his hand around it as he .... He ruthlessly cut off that particular thought as he closed the front door and made his way along the small hallway, to an open doorway on his left.

He stepped into a tiny, cosy living room, done in subtle shades of mocha and cream and russet. A small squashy, buttermilk leather sofa sat against the back wall and a single matching chair near the Alabaster fire place. A wood burning stove was lit in the fireplace giving off a relaxing glow and taking the chill out of the autumn air. His feet sank into a deep dark brown rug, placed in the middle of the room and covering a large section of the light wood flooring. Voile hung at the front window and he noticed that it had been artfully layered in several shades of mocha and cream. It showed off a sensuous side that she kept well hidden. He was just on his way to investigate several photographs on the fireplace that had caught his attention, when he heard her enter breathlessly behind him.

Kitty had rushed into her bedroom to pin her hair up and put her glasses on, she'd forgotten in her earlier rush to not keep Blake waiting on her doorstep. She was flustered after seeing him standing there dressed so casually. He was even more attractive in simple dark trousers and a white open necked shirt teamed with a lightweight black jacket.

He'd seemed larger than life standing on her doorstep and her heart had started up its now familiar and annoying rapid tattoo when in his company.

Cursing Audrey under her breath, as several sexual fantasies ran through her mind, with Blake, front and centre. If she'd just kept quiet earlier, none of these heated, arousing thoughts would be running rampant in her subconscious now. She was going to put salt in her coffee tomorrow and grinned at the thought as she tugged her hair into a slightly less severe style than she usually wore for work and slipped her glasses on. She pulled on a short black thigh length jacket and picked up a clutch bag, to match her black court shoes, a quick calming breath and she walked out of her room. Her step faltered as she saw where he was headed in the front room and coughed quickly to gain his attention. He turned to look at her and she watched his eyes lift to the top of her head and a frown furrow his brow.

Blake was disappointed to see that she'd pulled her hair up; not quite as severe as the style she wore for work, but it still gave off a "don't touch vibe" and he itched to reach out and pull it loose. Maybe run his fingers through it or and bury his face in the mass of silk, he shoved his hands in his pocket and he reminded himself to move gently, he'd get there one day, if he used baby steps and moved to join her.

Kitty saw a look of confusion cross his face and then clear as he flashed a quick smile and her pulse hammered as it joined her galloping heart, slamming against her ribs. The man was dangerous, gorgeous and her boss, she reminded herself as she turned towards the hallway to hide how flustered she was.

'I'm ready, didn't you say the table was booked for 8.45?' she babbled nervously to hide her reaction. 'To be honest I'm absolutely starving' she said opening the front door and waited for him to pass her. She'd needed to get him out of the house quickly, she'd forgotten about the photographs and could have kicked herself for the oversight. She would have to be more careful when he came again, then relaxed as she reminded herself that this visit was just a one off. A professional dinner date with a colleague, he wouldn't be coming to her home again.

She locked her door and dropped her keys into her bag then smiled stiffly at him as he held onto her elbow to help accompany her down the path. Her skin burning through her jacket at the contact and her stomach turned over, nervously. She was in deep trouble.

His new white range rover was parked just outside her gate and she watched in annoyance as blinds were moved over the road and groaned internally, it seemed Mrs Rawlings was awake and she would now find an excuse to come over in the next day or so to question her about her visitor. She scowled in her direction then schooled her features and chastised herself over the uncharitable thoughts running through her mind. She didn't mean anything by her nosiness, she was just lonely she reminded herself, and watching for gossip was her only source of entertainment. When she saw something, it gave her an excuse to knock and talk, that she could do without; not that Kitty would turn her away, she sighed. She just wished she wasn't so observant at this particular moment, she'd hound her for answers to questions she didn't have answers to herself.

She thanked him politely as he handed her into the car and waited while she got comfortable and did up her seat belt before closing the passenger door. He climbed in on his own side of the car and pressed the start button as he put his foot on the brake to engage the engine, the radio came on quietly in the background, as the car turned over. He pulled away from the curb, his lips twitching with amusement as he saw the gapped blinds drop back into place over the road.

'Interested neighbours, I see' he said with amusement, as he drove off up the street.

Blake spent the thirty minute journey doing his upmost to put Kitty at ease with small talk, not something he normally bothered with when on a date but this wasn't a normal date and he didn't like the way her knuckles whitened as they clutched onto the bag in her lap like a lifeline. He needed her to feel comfortable with him.

They discussed general topics like films and books and she was shocked to discover that they both had a love of action films and a secret passion for thrillers and Robin Williams's comedies.

He told her about growing up on a rough council estate and getting into trouble

'As boys do, although nothing too bad' he assured her. 'A bit of graffiti, giving the neighbours cheek, getting tattooed and staying out past curfew' he'd said then spoke of his mother Olivia with affection and explained about him and his sister taking after her for colouring and features.

'Mums tiny, just slightly over 5 feet, so obviously mine and Mel's height came from dad'. Then went on to tell her about his mother being widowed at 22 and being left to raise a 2 year old Blake and Melanie of only a few weeks old. He was quiet for a moment as he thought sadly of never really knowing his, "hero father", who'd given his life in service to his country. His mother had tried to keep him alive in their memory with stories and pictures over the years but it just hadn't been the same. He didn't explain that particular part though, not wanting so sound as if he was complaining, he wasn't. He'd just missed having a full time male influence around.

'He'd just gone back to duty after taking leave for Mel's birth, when the truck he was travelling in ran over a land mine', he said and heard her gasp. She squeezed his arm in sympathy, feeling for the children who'd lost their father at such a young age and their mother who'd lost her husband so tragically and so young.

He continued talking, ignoring her sign of support, needing to just finish telling her, he wasn't sure why he was telling her his life story? It wasn't something he ever usually spoke about.

'with mum at his side he died 5 days later in a military hospital due to complications of internal injuries and sepsis' he said but didn't tell her how devastated his mother had been for years afterwards that he'd never regained consciousness, so she'd never gotten over not being able to say goodbye' he couldn't tell her that.

He told her about the struggle she'd had raising them

'Mum wasn't qualified for much of anything and had to clean houses to make ends meet'. He didn't add that his father's pension had only been pennies, or that he had no life insurance or that they'd had to leave their home due to it being military married quarters. Or that he'd nearly worked himself into exhaustion doing 2 jobs as well as going through full time education to try and take some of the weight off his mother's shoulders.

'She's in a much better place now and extremely happy, funnily enough with one of dad's old army buddies who also happens to be our godfather' he added

'Greg Harrison kept me in line as best he could while I was growing up but he was never in one place long. He still served in the forces until 10 years ago, he came out after his wife became ill and took care of her for 3 years before losing her. After that he moved to be closer to us and the rest as they say is history' he told her

'Greg hasn't changed much over the years, he's slightly shorter than me but broader and he has the physique of a man much younger than his 58'. He laughed as he said 'you would not believe how shocked we all were when his military buzz cut grew out and all this thick chestnut hair appeared'. He shook his head at the memory 'He's a great guy, honest and intelligent and he has a wicked sense of humour. His qualities seem to complement and lighten mum's somewhat serious nature' he said but rushed on to explain

'Not that there was anything wrong her before, it's just she's been through a lot in her 51 years' he said

Kitty sat in quiet fascination as he regaled her with his family history it was a very private side to him that she'd never heard and quite honestly never expected to.

'We lived frugally but we knew we were loved' he said, a faint smile lifting one corner of his mouth.

'Greg was always in the background no matter where he was in the world or what was going on he never let one of our birthdays or Christmas go by without a visit or a card' he told her, genuine affection showing in his voice.

'He actually helped me get started, if not for him I'm not sure I'd be where I am today' or in such good mental health he thought but didn't say it. He'd been his rock when he'd desperately needed it over the years, his voice of reason and clarity when he was struggling with finding direction.

Kitty had been so engrossed in listening to Blake's talk, his voice although slightly rough had a soothing quality to it as he'd spoken at length. She'd been shocked to hear about his humble beginnings, especially when now, at only 32, he had an interest in several different businesses and a very impressive property portfolio.

She'd been really tense as they'd set out but as he'd opened up to her a little about his life, she'd found herself relaxing, so much so, that she now felt completely at ease with him. She no longer felt threatened by the tension between them and she turned her head to the side to look at him as he stopped talking and cleared his throat.

The car was quiet, too quiet, she couldn't even hear the engine ticking over and was shocked to realise that they'd stopped and she could see the hotel through the side window.

He grinned at her stunned expression as he pressed the stop button for the ignition and she looked from him to the hotel and back again.

'It looks rather sad at the moment doesn't it? But remember to keep an open mind, it's not always what it is but what it can be' as he jerked his head back towards the shabby but imposing building as he got out and moved around to help her.

Chapter Four

Blake was relieved to see that the smile she gave him this time was less reserved, the warmth reaching her eyes as he helped her out of the passenger side. She didn't even protest as he put his hands on her waist and lifted her down, her body brushing his and setting off little sparks. He liked how she felt against him and had to turn his head to stop himself from nuzzling her neck and inhaling her scent. It was different from what she usually wore, a little more exotic and he found it even more enticing than her day scent. She looked into his eyes and he saw a question there, as he didn't release her straight away, his hands still holding onto her waist, the pressure increasing slightly.

Kitty smiled her thanks as he bodily lifted her from the car, she'd relaxed in his company, probably too much she admitted as the heat of his hands settled on her waist. She had to fight the instinct to lean into him and take some of that warmth she could feel coming off his hard body, as he lifted her down. Her body slid deliciously down his length and she looked up at him confused as his hands tightened slightly on her before he moved her to the side, released her and stepped back slightly

'Pot whole' he said as way of explanation for his strange behaviour and was immensely pleased to see that there indeed was one. He placed his palm lightly on the small of her back, while he moved them forward. He kept it there as they walked side by side in companionable silence, he had to help her to step around several more pot holes as they made their way over the rather uneven and unkempt parking area.

They stopped in front of the impressive steps to the entrance and looked up at the, 6 storey high brownstone building set within a large piece of land. There was a wooded area to the left and rear, clearly visible with the outdoor lighting. The windows were arched but looked a little tired, the awning over the entrance had definitely seen better days and the brass handrail either side of the steps lacked lustre.

'Shall we?' he held his elbow out for her in an old courtly manner as they took their first step. She smiled her relief as she placed her hand through the crook of his arm as they made their way up, the steps were quite worn and uneven in places.

Once at the entrance, they walked through a large ornate glassed entrance and Kitty was immediately enveloped in a sense of old elegance, it had the feel of a bygone era about it.

As they stepped into the building she had a flash of the scene from Titanic; the one where Rose stood on the stairway. Straight ahead of them, at the back of the lobby, stood an ornate curved dark wood staircase that split off on a small landing.

It gave a view of the doors on the first floor landing through the intricate spindles. The lifts were on the right and the reception desk was on the left placed in between two doors. The carpet was a little shabby and the decorating needed to be modernized but all in all it was very appealing, it was full of charm and character.

Blake took her through the first open door they came to and they were greeted by a very statuesque, elegant blonde in a tight fitting, knee length, maroon cocktail dress. She stood to the side of a tall table with a reservation book placed on it. After taking their names and giving Blake a thorough once over, which instantly made Kitty scowl at how obvious she was in her interest. A waiter discreetly appeared to guide them to their seats. Blake kept his hand on the small of her back as they wove their way through diners to get to their table, it wasn't full but there were at least half of the tables taken.

Low jazz was filtered through the room and the buzz of conversation and cutlery was a soothing distraction in the background.

They were shown to a table in the left back corner behind a pillar, an intimate setting for 2 but with an excellent view of the kitchen door and bar area. The whole room was done in drab beige and the brass work again in here had also lost its lustre.

The carpet was a little sun damaged in places, due to the large windows along the side wall and the table linen was very plain and unimaginative. The silverware and glasses set out on the tables were not expensive examples but had been polished. Over all there was very little colour or warmth in the room apart from a red candle set in the middle of each table and although it did look very clean, the room wasn't very aesthetically pleasing.

The bar area looked like something out of the 1920's with a very heavy dark wood counter, with brass and lots of mirrors, the whole room definitely needed updating.

Kitty took her jacket off and placed it on the back of her chair after refusing the offer of the cloakroom, as did Blake. He rolled up his shirt sleeves, the action drew her eye to the fine sprinkle of hair covering his rather muscular tanned forearms and she found herself annoyed at noticing, especially as her interest was piqued as she spotted a small dark area that looked like a tattoo.

She cut off any thoughts of what it was and also wandering if he had that sprinkling of hair anywhere else.

The waiter leaned over and lit the candle in the middle of the table, gave them a food menu each, passed the drinks list to Blake then quietly left; giving them time to make their selections.

Blake looked up as the waiter left and was captivated by the blue highlights visible in Kitty's bound hair. He knew it was just because it was so black but as his eyes roved over her face his breath caught at her eyes. They sparkled like the purest cut emeralds behind her glasses, the gold flickering in their depths, the green blouse she wore was perfectly matched to them. He dropped his gaze as she caught him staring, her brow furrowing as her own gaze dropped down to her menu as she flicked through the selection. Her small white teeth tugging on her plump bottom lip took his attention away from her eyes as he watched her worry it.

The atmosphere at the table thickened as the relaxed mood from earlier fled and was replaced by awareness on both sides. Kitty racked her brain trying to think of something, anything to break the ice but her mind was still trapped on that dark ink and sprinkling of hair visible on his arms.

Blake cleared his throat and broke the weighted silence as he dragged his eyes away from her mouth.

'Would you like a drink while we decide on what to order?' he didn't much want a drink himself, or even food if he was being honest, he was much more interested in his companion. He just needed to say something to clear the sexual tension that had risen up between them. He needed her to relax with him, as she'd done earlier in the car, he'd notice her stiffened in her seat and cursed himself for not being able to control himself and staring at her. She was very intuitive though, it was as if she'd sensed danger, he'd felt the sexual tension building and crackling between them, just before she'd broken eye contact.

He watched as her brow wrinkled as she looked over towards the kitchen entrance, seemingly deep in thought. He'd bet his life she was trying to figure out a way to end the evening as quickly as possible. He just managed to stop the laugh building before it escaped, in the form of a cough. She really was unique and it would be a first for him if his female companion did a runner on him, never mind before they'd even ordered. He wasn't conceited but to be honest women were usually falling over themselves to get his attention, it was a novel situation he found himself in. Kitty wasn't getting away that easily, he could be tenacious when he wanted something and he desperately wanted her. He was just about to ask if there was a problem when she stood up distractedly.

'Excuse me for a moment' she said as she picked up her bag and went to move off, then turned back. 'Sorry, I won't be long, I just need to use the ladies room, could you order me a white wine spritzer please' she smiled absently at him and walked off.

He watched her walk back through the room and sullenly noticed several male eyes following her progress. She stopped to speak to the hostess before she moved out of the room and his sight. The waiter appeared at his side just as he was about to follow her, concerned that she was ditching him. He had visions of her ordering a taxi on her mobile, then shimmying out of the bathroom window. He was getting rather anxious over just that possibility when he spotted her jacket on the back of her chair and relaxed. She'd have to come back for that he assured himself, at least he hoped she would and scowled at the thought. The woman was tying him up in knots and he didn't like it in the slightest, he'd wanted a challenge but he at least would like to be on sure footing but with Kitty, that was not a certainty. The waiter approached and he shook himself out of the negative thoughts and asked for her requested drink and a small whisky for himself with a polite smile.

Kitty needed five minutes away from him to pull herself together, she was struggling keeping it polite and friendly, she stopped as the hostess looked towards her expectantly.

'I'm looking for the ladies room?' she said and the attractive blonde smiled and pointed her across from reception, towards the left hand side of the lifts under the staircase. She smiled her thanks and left hurrying towards her bolt hole, her heart racing and her hands becoming clammy in her agitation.

He'd been looking at her with lust in his eyes and she'd been tempted to lean towards him and take him up on his offer, what the hell was the matter with her? Surely she wasn't so stupid as to jump from one player to another. She needed her head examined she told herself as she looked into the mirror over the sinks, taking note of the high tell-tale colour in her cheeks. She shook her head in exasperation and ran her wrists under the cool water, hoping to alleviate the tension running through her body. She felt hot and achy, not a good way to be around a predator, he'd smell weakness and would use it to his advantage. She should know, she'd had enough dealings with his type over the years she thought bitterly. She just couldn't figure out his angle, he was oblivious to her family background so he must truly be interested in her but why? She went out of her way to play down her looks and had done since before she'd started to work for him, she couldn't figure out why after 2 years, she'd suddenly become "miss popular".

She needed to calm down, all he'd done was look, he hadn't made any untoward advances towards her or any lewd suggestions, she needed to chill out and calm down, she was behaving like a virgin in a brothel, she thought with disgust. She needed to pull up her big girl panties and get back in there, after all he was just a man, flesh and blood and she could handle him? "Yes you can, but can you handle yourself?" her subconscious said and she closed her eyes on the thought and took a couple of deep calming breaths. Her pupils were huge behind her glasses, she looked like she'd taken something illegal and she scowled at her reflection. She knew she was being ridiculous but she felt completely off kilter around him, he affected her more strongly than she would have believed possible. She blew out a breath, straightened her shoulders, dried her hands and left the relative safety of the ladies toilets.

She stiffened her spine as if she was "going in to battle", she thought a little hysterically. She knew she was over reacting, all they were doing was having dinner and discussing the merits of the place.

She needed to get a grip, he'd laugh if he could hear the panicked thoughts running through her head at the moment. She was making him out to be a modern day Casanova and everyone knew that you had to want to be seduced for the seduction to work and as she didn't, she was perfectly safe with him. Plus he was her boss and it would be unethical of him to hit on her she assured herself and that he wasn't, she was sure. Well she hoped, she'd never heard even a hint of office gossip about him with staff.

She realised she was mumbling to herself and looked around self-consciously at the other diners as she made her way grudgingly back to their table.

Blake looked up and smiled as she took her seat and she silently groaned. He really shouldn't smile at her, it did weird things to her stomach and it should be illegal she thought bitterly as she dropped back into her seat ungraciously. She grabbed the drink that was waiting for her, condensation running down the tall glass and took a large fortifying drink and smiled tentatively at him as he watched her with hungry hooded eyes. By the second sip she'd regained some of her fighting spirit and decided to play him at his own game.

She gave him her most coquettish smile, and fluttering her lashes; as she'd seen her mother do over the years, and watched with satisfaction as his eyes became shuttered. If he was going to play with her she was going to give him a run for his money she thought, taking another mouthful. Dutch courage could be a wonderful thing she thought with a sigh, another couple and she'd be absolutely fine and in control of the situation. She prayed.

Blake had ordered Kitties spritzer and had just taken a sip of his whisky while he perused the menu. He'd already decided what he wanted but he needed something to occupy himself, he was beginning to wonder if she had in fact bolted when she suddenly dropped down into her chair. She grabbed her drink and took a large swallow of the clear liquid, as if she'd been in the desert and was parched. He watched her cheeks flush with colour and her pupils dilate as their eyes met and he relaxed back into his seat, smiling at her knowingly as she gave him a shaky smile in return. He was feeling rather smug about the effect he had on when she gave him the most seductive smile he'd ever had, his heart actually missed a beat making him feel like bolting himself. A fine tremor began in his hands and he had to put his drink down before he spilt it.

'I really needed that' she said as she put down the half empty glass and picked up her menu as if she hadn't just knocked him on his arse; proverbially speaking of course. He was further shocked as she then calmly began to peruse the contents, her eyes moving slowly down the page as she read.

Warning bells were going off in his head. She knew what he was up to he realised in shock, her whole persona had changed from one of being cornered to one of strength and complete confidence in herself and the situation. His estimation of her intelligence, fire and backbone grew, she definitely had spirit and he really liked that, he didn't come across it too often, especially in women.

Well he had this morning, twice in fact, one he wasn't interested in though, she was old history. The other one was sitting across from him, her earlier anger had not been at him personally, just at the situation she'd walked in on and he'd happened to be in the firing line. He was either going to have to pull back and let it go, which he was loathed to do, or he was going to have to up his game.

Now that one had definite appeal he thought as he waited for her to decide what she was eating.

The rest of the meal was spent in general discussion on the latest book they were both reading, both warily avoiding anything remotely personal, as they seemed to circle each other testing for weaknesses as they ate their meal. They'd both ordered the same, the vegetable soup was delicious, thick and well-seasoned and the chicken was tender, the mashed potatoes creamy and the vegetables crisp and fresh.

Blake called for the bill as neither of them wanted dessert, they were both full after eating the delicious and well-presented but rather large portions of food. They decided by mutual consent to discuss their views of the place in the car on the journey home, they made general comments over the ambience and the food but anything in depth could wait for the journey home.

Blake paid the bill and they'd just got to his car when his phone went off, it was the call he'd been dreading about Melanie.

Chapter Five

Kitty leaned against his car and watched as his eyes grew warmer, a huge cat got the cream grin split his face, as he listened to whatever was being relayed to him. Obviously it was very good news and he was still smiling as he ended the call a few moments later and put his phone back in his jacket pocket. What she didn't expect was what came next.

Blake ended his call with Mike feeling lighter than he had in weeks. The worry over his sister on hold for now, the operation a success and he was so relieved he turned to Kitty, picked her up, swung her around and pinned her against his car as his mouth took hers. It was just meant to be an expression of his relief, a tentative peck to celebrate the good news, but he was not prepared for the sensation that slammed into him.

Their mouths touched and his brain short circuited as he went up in flames, electricity sparked and all his nerve endings lit up like a bonfire night fireworks display. He thrust his tongue in to taste her and was stunned to feel her own tongue brush against his. He pulled his head back in shock breaking contact about to apologise when he looked at her.

Her eyes were still closed, her long eye lashes fanning her flushed cheeks, mouth parted and wet from where he'd slid his tongue across the seam to open them. He meant to back off and go slow, he really did but the erotic vision before him just pushed all his buttons. He swooped back in just as her eyes started to flutter open and took them both to a place neither of them was prepared for.

Kitty was on fire, her body tingling everywhere they touched, she'd never felt anything like it, she needed to put a stop to this before it went somewhere she wasn't prepared to go but her body had other ideas. She melted into him, becoming pliant against his surprisingly hard chest as his grip on her waist became bruising as he plastered himself against her. She groaned in the back of her throat as his tongue once again swept inside her mouth, twisting and brushing over hers. She'd never felt anything as erotic as the mimicry of sex he was managing to produce with nothing but his mouth.

Her legs began to shake, she felt light headed as his mouth sipped from hers once more then slid down the side of her neck. He gave teasing nips and circled his tongue to sooth the sting before he sucked the sensitive skin between his talented lips.

She was in trouble, deep, deep trouble, he could take her now and she would be absolutely incapable of stopping him, would probably in fact be egging him on.

Blake needed to be inside her so badly, he was rock hard and aching, he could actually feel himself pulsing and straining against his zipper. He pushed against her trying to alleviate the ache as his mouth travelled over her tantalisingly supple neck. He had no idea where he was, nothing got through to his subconscious as it was wholly focused on Kitty and her addictive taste. She was molten heat in his arms as she leaned into him, her softness cushioning the hardness of his steel. His hands took on a life of their out as they roved over her body, they swept up from her wait to brush across her pebbled nipples through her blouse.

Kitty hissed at the light brush of his rough palm on her breast and reached blindly for him, thrusting her hands into his hair looking for an anchor as his mouth latched back onto hers. His palms brushed lightly back and forth across her sensitive nipples, she felt her womb contract, warmth pooling in her pelvis, as she felt his erection, like steel, flush against her stomach as he continued his twofold assault.

Their surroundings were completely forgotten in that moment when a high pitched wolf whistle sounded from nearby.

'Give her one for me' she heard, as if from a distance but the crude remark was enough to get through, like throwing cold water on her arousal. His as well if his reaction was anything to go by, he pulled back and turned, sheltering her with his body and she actually heard what sounded like a growl come from his throat. She was absolutely mortified by what she had just allowed to occur between them. She was so stupid, she knew he was dangerous, knew she needed to keep her guard up around him and could have cried. She was so embarrassed about the wanton way she had just behaved, it was so unlike her and all it had taken was a bloody kiss. She gulped in a lungful of cool evening air to clear the fog as she tried to drag together her shattered self-control, she was just about to push him from in front of her as he turned to look at her.

He ran his hand through his hair to bring it back into order, he needed to clear his head, god knows what would have happened if they hadn't been interrupted. He had never been so carried away and he didn't like it, no one before her had ever affected him to that extent where he became oblivious to his surroundings. He prided himself on his control in all situations but she'd shattered it with nothing more than a kiss.

He lifted his eyes to hers and was shocked to see her eyes shimmering with unshed tears, her throat working convulsively as she struggled with some inner turmoil. He lifted his hand trying to offer her comfort and winced as she flinched from his touch.

'Damn' he muttered as he stepped back, thrusting his hands in his pocket, 'I'm sorry Kitty' he said struggling to find a reason for the extraordinary response she'd pulled from him. She looked at him with steely resolve, her back straightening and her slightly tipped nose lifting minutely as she thrust her small chin out in defiance. He wanted to grin at the picture of pique she presented but knew it would be a really, really bad idea.

'I think it's time I took you home' he said instead and reached around her to open the passenger door. She refused his proffered hand and struggled into her seat, eyes fixed ahead through the windshield as he closed her door. He moved slowly around and opened his own door wincing at the discomfort from his still semi hard erection as he sat down. He would have loved nothing more than to rearrange himself into a more comfortable position but didn't think she'd appreciate it. He grit his teeth and pulled the door closed and fastened his seat belt. As the engine sprang to life he laughed out loud when the first sound out of the radio was Marvin Gaye's 'sexual healing'. He was helpless to control the amusement bubbling up, just a knee jerk reaction to the whole sorry situation.

He looked over to Kitty and saw her shoulders shaking, he was concerned, had he frightened or upset her. When her hands lifted and covered her face he became even more concerned until she let out a real belly laugh as her head leaned back against the head rest. He relaxed, shaking his head at the absurdity of it, the awkward tension broken as he drove away from the hotel and the scene of his downfall. He needed to get her away from there quickly before he did something else completely out of character, liked pulling over and ravishing her on the side of the road.

The return journey to her home was completed in silence, neither of them seemed willing to speak.

Kitty had been angry and then mortified in turn by the stupid song coming on the radio but it had lightened the mood, helping to dispel the sexual tension. She had had to see the funny side of it, she really did or she'd cry from sexual frustration. She just wanted to get home and forget about the whole thing.

Blake pulled up outside her flat without looking her way and sat patiently waiting for her to leave.

'I don't think it would be wise for me to walk you to your door' he told her looking through the windshield, his knuckles white as they gripped the steering wheel to stop himself from reaching for her.

'I appreciate that' she told him as she pushed the door open and jumped down. 'I enjoyed the meal and company' she informed him and her face flushed as his hooded blazing eyes turned on her 'well until the end' she added and his mouth twisted cynically.

'You and I both know I could prove you wrong on that score' he informed her and watched in satisfaction as her cheeks flushed as she turned away. 'Goodnight Kitty, see you in the morning' he said 'we still need to discuss the hotel' he reminded her. He had visions of her disappearing and he wanted to let her know that it would be business as usual in the morning. She nodded her ascent so he'd let things lie for now, but he couldn't guarantee for how long, his libido ramped up every time he so much as thought of her.

'Goodnight Mr Dennison' she replied as she closed the door, he shook his head at her as she walked up the path. Damn he loved her fighting spirit, letting him know that as far as she was concerned, any personal feelings were being left here and now.

"We'll see Kitty" he said to himself as he watched her disappear from view behind her closed front door and drove away, it was going to be a cold shower and a long night for him.

Kitty walked through the flat and straight into her bedroom, stripped off her clothes, pulled on an overlarge t-shirt and stepped into the bathroom. She looked critically at her reflection, her eyes were huge and haunted and her mouth was swollen and bruised.

She removed her glasses and washed her mascara off but didn't need to bother with the removal of her lip gloss; Blake had seen to that and groaned. She scowled at her reflection and refused to dwell on what had happened after the meal, she needed to forget for her own peace of mind. She brushed her teeth and turned off the light.

She crawled into bed pulling the duvet up to her chin as she waited for sleep to claim her. She could still smell him, his scent seemed to have soaked into her pores and she buried her face in her pillow and groaned as she willed herself to relax and sleep. When it finally came, her dreams were vivid, erotic and starred he who should not be named.

Chapter Six

Kitty woke feeling thoroughly rested and optimistic as the alarm roused her from her dream lover's embrace. She hopped out of bed and headed for a quick shower, today was a new day and she was going to put last night behind her she promised herself. She would show a professional, pleasant front and behave as if nothing untoward had happened between them. Blake was probably suffering some misgivings himself this morning she soothed herself and she refused to allow sexual chemistry to dictate her actions. She was a grown up and life was about more than sex, well it always had been up until now, but she pushed that negative thought aside.

Blake was in a foul mood as he arrived in the office, he was late and frustrated as hell. He'd taken two cold showers, even taken matters into his own hands at one point, so to speak but the damn thing kept standing to attention every time he thought about the damn woman. He had to get her into bed and under him soon, he needed some peace and a restful night's sleep. He scowled at Audrey as he passed her desk.

'Morning Blake, good night was it?' she asked sweetly as she grinned and returned to her work. He grunted at her as he stormed into his office and slammed the door.

'Bloody woman' he said under his breath, if she wasn't so good at her job he'd have snapped at her but then again she'd have just laughed at him, she didn't scare. She was probably bullet and fire proof too, he thought uncharitably.

His door opened just as he sat down and Audrey appeared with a cheery smile and placed a steaming cup of coffee down in front of him.

'That'll help cure what ails you' she winked at him cheekily as she left the room. He groaned and dropped his head down onto his hands in frustration, how the bloody hell could he have let his interest in a woman do this to him. God she would pay when he finally got her naked and underneath him he promised himself. That thought cheered him somewhat as he sat up and took a sip of the hot, strong brew with a sigh, he needed to put her out of his mind and get on with business.

Kitty sailed out of the lift and smiled broadly at Audrey as she got an empty cup and poured coffee into it.

'Want one?' she asked as she added milk and sugar to her own and stirred as Audrey lifted up her own cup to show her she was fine as she typed one handed. Kitty picked up her own doctored cup and went to her desk, dropping down with a grin as she took a sip and sighed in pleasure

'Isn't it a lovely day?' she said as Audrey snorted and carried on typing.

'I take it you didn't jump him?' she said to Kitty, 'he's acting like a bear with a sore head' she continued, trying to work out what had gone on between them but Kitty kept her head down and Audrey continued 'and you're walking around like little miss sunshine' she announced as she looked at her critically over her cup. Her brow furrowed as she took in Kitty's flushed cheeks and the way her eyes avoided hers and burst out laughing.

'He tried didn't he?' he said in glee as Kitty sputtered indignantly at her 'he did and you knocked him back' she added as she thought about her and Blake's demeanours. 'Oh it's going to be fun around here' she added with a wide knowing grin as she went back to work humming happily to herself.

'I don't know what you're talking about?' Kitty sniffed indignantly as she booted up her computer and put her coat behind her.

'Oh yes you do and you do also realise that you've just set yourself up as a challenge don't you?' Audrey asked and grinned as Kitty's eyes opened wide but there was no time to answer as Blake appeared at his door.

'Kitty a word please' he said and walked back inside.

'Ooh better tighten that chastity belt my girl' Audrey shouted after her as she moved towards his office.

'Oh bite me, you witch' Kitty hissed over her shoulder as she disappeared into his office to the sound of Audrey's laughter and just caught.

'Nah, he'll be biting you' between bouts of laughter as the door closed on her.

Kitty turned from closing the door trying to school her features as Blake sat behind his desk tapping his pen in agitation.

'What was all that about?' he asked watching her face flush

'What the hell did you say?' she spat at him as she stormed towards his desk.

'I've not said a bloody thing' he growled at her as he stood up and moved around his desk, stalking her, she back tracked as she suddenly realised she'd just poked the tiger. What was the matter with her? She was usually better at keeping her temper under control but he seemed to bring out the worst in her, or at least he did lately.

Unlike the last time though, Blake kept coming, as she moved around the chair and rushed back to the door, looking for safety with Audrey. He was quicker though, his hand coming over her head and slamming it against the door to keep it closed. He had her pinned against the cool wood, his chest flush against her back. She sucked in a shocked breath as arousal slammed violently into her. His scent enveloped her and every breath he took she felt run through her. She closed her eyes and tried to take shallow breaths to put some space between them. Her anxiety levels rising along with her temper as she felt threatened by the sexual tension, thick in the air.

'Move' she hissed pushing back against him trying to give herself breathing room and gasped as she felt his arousal brush up against her bottom.

Blake didn't know how this had started but he was bloody well going to finishing it, he was not going to have a repeat of last night.

He left one hand against the door, to keep it closed and raised the other one to her chin so he could turn her slightly, then lowering his mouth to her ear, he whispered

'You started this' pushing into her again so she would feel his arousal, his breath washing over her and making her squirm as he pushed softly against her

'I only think it's fair that you help me alleviate the discomfort this time' he said as he nibbled on her ear lobe then ran his tongue around the shell as his hand moved slowly down to her throat, his thumb brushing over the frantically beating pulse there. She closed her eyes and desperately tried to fight the pull, she'd had such high hopes when she'd come in a few minutes ago. How stupid she was thinking the kind of chemistry running between them could just be swept under the carpet. She had never known it this strong before. Sex wasn't something she was really interested in, although she did enjoy cuddling.

'But I don't even like sex' she whispered on a gasp as he tugged her lobe with his teeth and he laughed huskily. Oh he was going to enjoy rectifying that situation.

'What sort of idiot's have you been dating?' he drawled, enjoying her indignant gasp. He grinned wickedly as he slowly turned her to face him, taking great pleasure in her flushed face and dilated, glazed eyes.

He backed her against the door again this time chest to chest and removed her glasses, then grinned and tutted as he realised they were made of clear glass. He shook his head in mock regret as he threw them to the side and raised his hands to her hair. His mouth captured hers as she took a breath to speak, his tongue rasping along her teeth before he sucked her own questing tongue into his mouth and shivered as she groaned against him, swallowing the sound.

He began blindly pulling pins from her hair, dropping them by his feet one by one, until the curtain of long black silk brushed over his hands and arms. He pulled back to stare at his handy work, his breath catching in his lungs as he watched her through heavy lidded eyes. She was breath taking, he just needed a moment to take her in and mentally catalogue the changes. Her hair hung down over her shoulders in loose waves, a curtain of living, vibrant silk and that snapshot of memory surfaced and vanished again before he could he could grasp it. He brushed his nose against all the glorious treasure he revealed, inhaling deeply before nudging it to the side as his mouth sought the delicate, sensitive skin at her throat.

'Oh god' was the only coherent word she could form before her brain shut down as she was bombarded with pleasure, turning her into a mass of pure need. His hands and mouth left a trail of fire everywhere they touched. Her body ached and wept for him at the same time, her womb contracted, her breasts became heavy, her nipples tight, aching buds. 'We shouldn't be doing this' she managed to get out on a whisper

'Then tell me to stop' he groaned as he ran his tongue down her throat, quickly popping the buttons on her blouse, giving him further access. He continued to lick and kiss downwards, then over the swell of her breasts, the only sound she could manage was a groan as she lifted her hands into his hair to anchor him to her, as she urged him on with needy little moans.

He responded to her complete surrender with a shudder as he ground himself against her, letting her feel how hard and thick he was and how badly he needed inside her. His hand trailed up her leg, pushing her skirt higher and higher, then groaned again as his fingers brushed over smooth soft skin as her stockings ended. He slid a knee between her legs parting her thighs to make a cradle for himself, then pressed himself against her to try and assuage the ache in his groin. He tugged her bra cup below her breast and lowered his mouth to suckle her distended nipple.

She dropped her forehead onto his shoulder, too overwhelmed by the sensations bombarding her to hold her own weight, she nuzzled into his neck as he ground against her. It was too much, she turned her head and bit down through his shirt and into his shoulder to muffle the sob that left her. She scored her nails down his back and arched against him.

The sensation of pleasure pain she produced with both her mouth and nails was electrifying and he lost control completely, releasing her nipple and lifting her bodily against the door

'Wrap your legs around my waist' he managed through clenched teeth, as he picked her bodily up, his hands a death grip on her rounded bottom and holding her flush against him. He began to move blindly across the office with her wrapped around him, he took her mouth again deepening the kiss as he lowered her onto the couch in the corner and came down on top of her. They were both fully clothed, her breast on display as her blouse fell back, his shirt was partly undone and his tie was skewwhiff from where her hungry hands pushed it impatiently out of her way to roamed over his hair roughened chest before moving up and fastening behind his neck. Her mouth left his and she trailed teasing kisses along his throat and bit down where it joined his shoulder, making him groan as he thrust against her reflexively. He needed to slow it down and get her out of her clothes, he wanted to take his time and explore every piece of skin he exposed.

Kitty had other ideas as he tried to put some room between them so he could undress them both, she wrapped her legs tightly around his back and arched and rubbed the neediest part of her against his erection. He swooped down and suckled her breast as he ground back against her rubbing himself against the tight bundle of nerves in her sex and they both groaned in unison at the shocking sensation. Her nipple slipped from his mouth with a pop as he ground helplessly against her. She let loose a low keening moan at the movement, the hair rising on the back of his neck at the sound and he took her mouth to silence her.

That sound was the final thread snapping for him, he was about to burst, he thrust against her blindly, trying to enter her, through both sets of clothes. The breathy moans and the way she rubbed against him drove him absolutely wild and he groaned again, as she gasped and went stiff beneath him as she found her release. He was helpless to do anything but follow her over, throwing back his head in ecstasy, grinding his teeth as his neck muscles strained and he shuddered through the longest release he'd ever had before collapsing boneless and weak on top of her still shaking form.

They lay tangled together gasping for breath, sweat beaded on his forehead as his heart beat out a rapid tattoo in his chest, before slowing back down. He sighed in contentment and felt Kitty stir beneath him and lifted up slightly on his elbows to take his weight off her and gauge her reaction. Her hair billowed out over his arms and the couch and flowed onto the floor, her eye lids were at half mast, her mouth swollen and her face and chest flushed with colour. He felt smug pride fill his chest, knowing that he'd done that to her, made her look so thoroughly satisfied, dazed and ravished. He bent forward needing to taste her again, a smile playing at the corner of his mouth but before their lips connected, she moved and he got a mouthful of couch.

'Move' she hissed, pushing her closed fists against his chest with such force, he fell on the floor in a confused heap at the unexpected action. She leapt off the couch, tugged her bra back over her breast, pulled her blouse together and fastened it with shaking hands before pushing her skirt down. Her fingers brushed her hair out of her eyes as she looked around the floor for the pins that had been holding it in a tight chignon.

He was still slightly sluggish from satisfaction, his brain not working at full capacity.

She dropped to her hands and knees frantically picking up her hair pins and looking for her glasses as panic began to set in, she needed to get out. She was mortified at what had just happened, what she'd allowed to happen. She didn't fool herself, she knew she'd fully participated and thoroughly enjoyed it, had been stunned by the pleasure as a matter of fact. She had the first orgasm of her life, well awake anyway she admitted and her body hummed in memory, desperate to experience it again. She was ashamed, maybe he wasn't as bad as she'd originally thought but he was still a womanizer, he thought nothing of sex with no strings but then what did that make her as she'd just allowed it. Well maybe he'd not had her body fully, there'd been no penetration but he'd played it like a master and you didn't get that good without lots of practice, she thought bitterly. She'd be damned before she let it happen again.

Blake pulled himself upright just as Kitty rushed into his private bathroom and slammed and locked the door behind her. He ran his hand over his face to try and clear it, his blood still not reaching his brain properly and hauled himself wearily to his feet before going over to tap on the door.

'Open up Kitty, we need to talk'

'Not gonna happen' came the sharp reply.

Her voice was muffled as she had hair pins in her mouth as she pulled her hair frantically back into order and clipped it into place. She washed her hands and face, noticing her sparkling eyes and flushed cheeks in the mirror and pulled out her tongue childishly at her reflection. Hissing with annoyance, she slipped her glasses back on. Her body felt sated and she was completely livid with herself.

'Come on Kitty, we need to talk about the hotel' Blake wheedled from outside the door trying to get her out. 'Audrey's going to wonder what's taking so long' he said knowing that would get her moving like nothing else could. Audrey was as straight as they came and she wouldn't think twice about interrogating her and he grinned at the thought. Sobering quickly as he nearly fell through the open doorway he was leaning against as she pulled the door open and stood there, hands on hips, scowling at him. He scowled right back annoyed that she'd put the disguise back in place with the professional glasses covering her eyes again. He was even more annoyed that she'd tightly pinned all that glorious hair up again and lifted a hand to pull the pins out again but she slapped at it.

'Don't' she snapped as her hand and eyes lowered and blurted 'oh for god sake, change your pants' and she slipped around him, her nose in the air. He watched her tiredly as she dropped down into the chair in front of his desk, crossing one leg over the other as she clasped her hands in her lap and she waited for him to comply.

He looked down at the dark wet patch visible in his light grey suit pants and winced, ran his hand through his hair and took his turn in the bathroom. He'd burned the midnight oil frequently in the early days, sleeping on his office couch, so luckily out of habit he always kept spare clothes on hand.

Kitty was humiliated by what had just happened, I mean she'd walked in on something similar only yesterday in Lance's office. Maybe it was expected and she'd just been too stupid, or too naïve to realise it. Then she sobered as she admitted she was being overly critical of Blake, he hadn't forced her, he'd given her a choice, even going so far as to asking her to tell him to stop. She bit her lip, raised a hand and smacked her forehead with her palm.

'Stupid, stupid, what were you thinking?' she asked herself out loud.

'I don't think much thinking was going on' Blake said dryly from behind her as he came out of the bathroom and watched in amusement as she jumped in her chair. She'd been so deep in thought she hadn't even heard him open the door.

'Let's just forget about that shall we' she told him as he moved around his desk and took his seat.

'You can't be serious?' he said incredulously, running his hand through his damp hair

'I'm deadly serious' she snapped and dropped her eyes as she clasped and unclasped her hands in agitation. She cleared her throat and chanced a look at his face. His hair looked darker damp and had become dishevelled as he brushed it impatiently off his face with a hand.

His eyes followed her every movement like a hawk, she could practically hear the cogs turning, as he tried to figure out a way to make her change her mind. That was never going to happen, as if she was going to touch that one she thought and rolled her eyes at the ridiculousness of it. She was not stupid, she knew he could be dangerous to her in more ways than she was even willing to admit, she cleared her throat again and quickly tried to distract him from his train of thought.

'You wanted to discuss the hotel?' she said schooling her features.

Blake watched in fascination as her usually expressive face became a polite, competent mask and he didn't like it, not one bit, he wanted her back to moaning and writhing beneath him, preferably naked this time. He wanted to see her passion and feistiness return, he despised the professional mannequin that she had turned into in front of him now and cursed his libido under his breath. So much for finesse, he'd rushed in like an inexperienced teenager and she'd back pedalled in panic at the passion that had ignited between them. The chance of getting any further in being able work her out of his system was looking decidedly grim. The problem was he found that now he had seen all that hidden passion he wanted to see it again and again. She kept him mentally and physically on his toes and he couldn't remember that ever happening before with any other woman. He gave her a small polite smile as he forced himself to relax back in his chair, he could be as remote as her he thought. Let's see how she liked being kicked to the back burner, as if a temporary insanity had been satisfied but was too distasteful to be repeated.

'As you wish, take it as forgotten' he informed her magnanimously with a wave of his hand and turned to his computer as he opened up the e-mail she'd forwarded him with her recommendations. He watched in silent amusement as her luscious mouth compressed, her brow furrow and her eyes behind those hideous thick rimmed glasses lit with indignation at his easy compliance and had to suppress a grin. 'Gotcha' he thought smugly and quickly read through her views.

Kitty sat silently fuming in the chair opposite him, she was positively vibrating with annoyance. How dare he treat the single, most satisfying sexual experience she'd ever had, as if it had meant absolutely nothing. Who the hell did he think he was? How dare he treat her feelings with such disregard, she could feel her hackles rising at his dismissive behaviour, then reminded herself that she'd been the one that had requested he did so. It was just his easy acceptance of it still stung and she wasn't sure she could let it go.

She took a deep breath and opened her mouth ready to give it to him with both barrels when she looked up. She noticed the cynical little twist to his lips, the laughter playing at the back of his eyes and snapped her mouth shut again. 'Ah' he was playing her, well wasn't that interesting, two could play at that game she thought and forced herself to relax nonchalantly back into her own chair, and forcing herself to stop twisting her hands in agitation.

A line appeared between his brows and she mentally sighed as she ticked a point for her and had to suppress a giggle.

Blake turned his head from the screen after reading through the detailed recommendation's she'd entered as Audrey knocked and entered.

'I thought you could do with some sustenance as you've been so busy, you've been locked in here for ages' she added with an innocent expression as she placed a tray of coffee and a plate of biscuits between them. She smiled sweetly at Blake and gave Kitty a shit eating grin as she left again, whistling to herself as she closed the door. Both Blake and Kitty sighed and picked their respective cups up.

'Do you think she knows what we've been up to?' Blake asked her as he bit into a digestive with a grin and nearly choked at the horrified expression that crossed Kitty's face. All her colour had drained and she had to hold her cup with both hands, they were shaking so badly she nearly dropped it. 'Audrey won't say a word' he rush on trying to reassure her when she spluttered hostilely

'As you're so sure of her discretion, it makes me wonder how often it's had to come into play' she remarked bitterly and he slammed his cup down.

'I resent that remark' he snapped at her 'you really have a low opinion of me don't you?' he said and watched the colour leach from her face as she realised her barb had hit.

'I have never had sexual relations with any of my employees' he then added 'You are an anomaly', as his eyes roamed broodily over her face, he was unhappy to find himself in this untenable situation to begin with. A first for him, but due to the extraordinary chemistry between them, he wasn't backing down, he wanted to glut himself on the passion that sprang between them. He was also extremely relieved to see colour flood her cheeks, it seemed that both of them were on shaky ground, her embarrassed blush showing him that she wasn't as confident about his disreputable character as she'd like him to believe.

Kitty was horrified that she'd once again verbally assaulted him without any real provocation, what the hell was the matter with her? She seemed to have no filter between her brain and her mouth around him recently

'I'm sorry, that was uncalled for' she said sheepishly as she took a sip of coffee 'but let's face it, you can hide in here but I have to sit across from her' she shuddered as he burst out laughing at her dramatics and lifted his cup up to take another drink, his annoyance evaporating as fast as it had risen as he relaxed again.

'Audrey may be a pain in the arse at times but she's harmless, priceless and completely discrete, nothing will leave these walls' he assured her and watched with satisfaction as her expression began to thaw.

It seemed they were back on safe ground again.

Blake would miss her when this ended, as all his affairs did. He would eventually lose interest and then they would just go their separate ways but the thought of not seeing, touch or verbally sparring with kitty left him feeling quite queasy. What on earth was the matter with him, maybe he'd eaten something last night that didn't agree with him, had given him this sick feeling in the pit of his stomach. It certainly couldn't be the thought of never again having Kitty spit and scratch at him, once it was over, could it? He threw that thought away, refused to look closely at it, he didn't get attached to his lovers, ever. He was being preposterous, he was just sorry that he'd have to find another Personal Assistant when this was over, that's all.

Chapter Seven

They spent the next hour or so going over the finer details of the hotel purchase, including the debt amount that was outstanding on Jake Masterson's loan. They speculated at how legal the fine print and clauses were in the contract was with reference to the exorbitant interest payments and stipulations that Jake Masterson's backer had included

'I'll get in touch with the legal department before I have lunch' Blake said 'I want to put an offer in for the outright purchase of the hotel' and Kitty raised an eyebrow

'Do you really think it's worth it?' she looked down at the figures 'that's an awful lot of zero's' she added and Blake grinned.

'I have a really good feeling about the place, I'm aware it's going to take a lot of money to bring it to life and update it, but my gut tells me it'll be well worth it in the long run'. He sat back invigorated about the whole thing. This was exactly what he'd been looking for, extensive grounds, no major planning problems with the greenbelt attached; not that he would be touching the wooded area surrounding it.

He had some plans for the place, he was going to take it up market, bring it into the 21st century and the challenge was just what he thrived on.

Kitty watched his face animate as he began to explain his plans, he oozed intelligence and enthusiasm as he described his visions for the renovation in minor detail. He pulled out the blue prints and spread them on the floor in front of him, motioning her over to have a look.

'Do you know how to read these?' he asked as she settled on her knees beside him and studied the bold black lines on the paperwork. It was cut into sections showing detailed sizes and dimensions of each room, height and floor space, it was huge, even had a full size cellar.

'Wow, you could put a modern bar and dance area down there, live unsigned music nights are hugely popular at the moment' she said, his enthusiasm catching. 'There would also be room to add a gym and massage area' she added as she ran her hand over the plans.

Blake watched Kitty as she took in all the information and pointed.

'Look at the back there, they have a substantial conservatory that's being used as a breakfast area' she looked up at him to make sure he was listening.

'A swimming pool would be great there instead, the size is good and you'd be able to fit in a changing area' she said running her fingers over the layout 'The wooded areas could be utilized as wild walks' she added 'and the area to the side could be set up as a child's adventure area' she could visualize the changes in her head.

Blake was astounded at her grasp and imagination, it was fascinating to watch how her brain worked and she had some damn fine ideas. He rolled up the blue prints and stood up, holding his hand out to her.

'Come on, time for lunch' he said 'I need to make some calls, it's time to put Jake out of his misery' he added as she placed her hand in his trying to ignore the electricity that ran up her arm as he tugged her to her feet. He didn't release her hand straight away but stood holding it while he looked seriously at her. 'This thing between us isn't going to just go away' he told her, one finger running lightly down her cheek and watched in rapt attention as her eyes closed at the intimate touch.

That fast he was hard again and gave into temptation as he gave her a chaste kiss, their lips barely touching. A soft inhalation from her as he held the contact for only a fraction of a second before he pulled back. He suppressed a groan as her heard her sigh, releasing her hand with a squeeze.

'I won't lie, I'd like to see where this takes us?' he said with a rueful smile

'But that decision is yours to make Kitty' he put his hands in his pockets and stepped back to put some distance between him and the temptation she presented.

'I'm not Edmondton' he said 'and I promise you that although my affairs are usually short, they're always monogamous' he added as he moved towards the door but before he opened it he said

'Think about it, we would be very good together' and with that opened the door and watched as she moved quietly past him to her own work space, seemingly deep in thought. He smiled ruefully to himself as he closed the door, he felt like a heel using his experience against her but nowhere near enough to back off, he wanted her too badly to worry about ethics.

He moved back to his desk and called his legal department on the floor below requesting them to get the ball rolling. He'd speak to Jake after lunch he decided catching the time, he'd told his mother he'd pop in for lunch today. He grabbed his suit jacket and walked out, deliberately averting his eyes from Kitty.

'I'm off for lunch' he announced, just as the lift door closed on him.

Kitty was deep in thought as he passed her desk and didn't look up as he left. She was still hearing his parting words in the office, as they played on a loop in her head. Could she really have a no strings affair with him? Would she survive it? Damn it she was confused, although her body was definitely on board with the idea, it practically hummed in remembrance of the satisfaction it had received earlier, at his hands.

'He'd be good for you' Audrey piped up from her desk and Kitty bit her lip in indecision as she looked up at her. Audrey sighed, 'he's not another Lance' she said in exasperation 'he may not be perfect but he's a good man' she added 'and just think about the sex' her eyebrows waggled suggestively 'don't discount amazing sex my girl' she said watching the colour bloom in Kitty's cheeks and laughed 'ooh already had a taste have we' she said and then sighed as Kitty lost colour. 'Look I've worked with Blake for a few years now and I've never once seen or heard any whispers of him messing around with the staff' she informed her and Kitty looked sceptical at that.

'What if I can't do the no strings thing?' she asked

'Everyone goes into relationships blindly, no one knows how things are going to work out. But ask yourself this, are you willing to walk away from something that could be good for you simply because you've already decided it's going to end?' Kitty thought about what had happened earlier, how Blake had made her feel and looked back at Audrey.

'I'm scared' she admitted biting her lip

'Sweetie, we all are at some point, but if you allow that fear to rule you' her shoulders lifted in a negligent shrug, 'you could end up losing out on something special. Look at me, 'I didn't know where things were going to go when I started to date Dan' she said 'He was an exciting vibrant artist for god sake and I was this dowdy Admin Assistant, two complete opposites' she smiled 'but you know what? He made me feel alive in ways no one else ever had' she added 'he made me feel special and oh my god, the sex was amazing' she said with a chuckle.

'Passion doesn't last' Kitty huffed

'No, not the madness it starts out as' she agreed 'but given time it becomes something more, tender and enriching, giving you both emotional stability with someone who really knows you'

'But what if it doesn't work out, what then?' she whispered

'Then you have some great memories' she said 'now come on, my shout at the café' she said as she put the calls on re-route through to the main reception and grabbed her coat.

They put their order through at the counter and Audrey paid while Kitty grabbed a window table. The food was excellent here and not overly expensive, they had their usual dish of Lasagne with a side salad and shared some warm crusty bruschetta. Kitty ate with relish and felt better after she'd finished. They sat back as the table was cleared and a tall latte was put down for each of them.

'Thanks' Kitty smiled at Beth, their usual waitress as she left them in peace to finish. This had become a kind of ritual for them, a way to unwind and regain their stamina for the final shove towards the weekend. Their version of a hump day. Audrey watched Kitty over the top of her cup, she could see the cogs turning, which was good as it meant she was thinking about it.

'Dan has a small art exhibit on Saturday' she said 'how about you come along and I'll invite Blake' she added and rushed on before Kitty could refuse, 'just an informal get together in a relaxed non-threatening environment, maybe it will help you make up your mind?' she said

'I've already been with him in a relaxed environment remember, the hotel dinner?' she said and Audrey's face split into a huge toothy grin, then laughed 'now how could I forget that after the fireworks it started' then sobered as Kitty's brow furrowed and sighed 'Look I know you're concerned about his casual reputation but do you really want to wake up one day 20 years from now and wonder what might have been?' she added. 'Plus 30% of any sales or commissions Dan gets are going to the spinal research charity, so it's for a good cause. You should come for that alone' she added as she finished her coffee.

Now how could Kitty refuse that, she had her over a barrel and by the satisfied smile on her face she knew it too. She was a devious woman, she probably ran rings around poor Dan but what she said made sense. Did she really want to play it safe and miss out on something that had the potential to bring her immeasurable pleasure? Or did she just want to sit on the side lines and watch the procession of women he dated start up again?

Could she handle a no strings affair? Just go with the flow and see where it took her, she found her interest piqued at the possibilities that brought, long leisurely nights of satisfied entwined limbs.

The only problem was, she had major trust issues, not without reason she assured herself but Blake was wealthy and successful in his own right, he didn't need to be devious and influence her to try and get to her parents for his further gain. He wasn't even aware of who she really was, no one at work was. Maybe she should rectify that first, after all, if they were going to do this she wanted to start off with a clean slate. She hoped that if she was up front and honest from the beginning it would stop any nasty surprises from cropping up later on.

She just wanted to be wanted for herself not what people thought her parents could do for them, was that so bad? Also if she didn't do this, could she continue to work for him if she was constantly?

dealing with the hordes of woman who would gladly take her place?

She was surprised to find that the thought of him with anyone else made her slightly nauseous and roused her jealousy. That was a new emotion for her, she'd never been jealous of anyone before. That was not good a good omen, it didn't bode well for keeping things light. She bit her lip in indecision.

'Oh for god sake stop over analysing everything and just go with the flow' Audrey advised as she got up and dropped a tip on the table. They walked back to work arm in arm, Kitty shivering as she huddled into her thin coat. Audrey kept up a steady flow of chatter as she told her about the new pieces that Dan had completed.

'He's finished some small sculptures and I think you'll really like them' she said as the lift took them back to their floor.

****

Blake had a leisurely lunch with his mum and Greg. He loved the new house Greg had moved into with his mother, open spaces, a great view and a huge old farmhouse kitchen. He visited at least once a week for a catch up and to check that everything was okay, an old habit he'd been unable to shake. He spoke to them at length about his interest in the Bellville hotel and the problems the owner had been having with his backer. Greg sat back in his seat and tapped his fingers against his cup, his other arm around the back of Olivia's chair as he absently ran his fingers up and down her arm.

'Bellville?' he said 'just off the beaten track outside Wilmslow, a little run down, good sized property and land with a wooded area?' he asked

'Yes, that's the one, have you seen it?' he asked and Greg shook his head

'Not personally but I have an acquaintance who's a property valuation expert, he recently did a detailed report on it for a local asset stripper'. His eyebrows lowered in a frown as he concentrated on something then lifted and smoothed out as he clicked his fingers in remembrance, 'Lance Edmonton'. Blake's own brows rose so high in surprise at the name that they almost disappeared into his hair line.

'Edmonton, what's his interest in the property?'

'He's the backer for the Bellville but he wants the property badly for himself now. He's hoping to receive an exorbitant sum for the land from interested foreign parties' Greg added. The cogs in Blake's head started to turn, he'd been interested in this property for a while and he had the nasty suspicion that Lance had known. He'd bet his fortune that he'd targeted Kitty specifically to get to him, but why? His anger rising on her behalf, he felt physically sick, she was going to be devastated when he told her. Then thought better of it, it was only supposition on his part and did she really need to know?

It wouldn't achieve anything other than to make her feel even more foolish. She'd seen him for the prick he was and had already dumped him. Surely he wouldn't hold any interest to her now the blinkers were off? He stopped his musings as he caught sight of the time on his wristwatch over the rim of his cup. He quickly swallowed the dregs at the bottom. He needed to get back to the office and get the various departments moving on this deal, pronto, he had no time to waste.

All in all this lunch had been illuminating in more ways than one. They were all going to get together in a week or two, the whole family for a celebratory meal once Mel was back on her feet. They were all relieved and quietly optimistic that she'd gotten through the critical 24 hour danger time and were hoping the twin girls were going to be fine. Mike was just being overly protective at the moment, not that he could blame him. She needed a couple of extra days bed rest before he'd let her travel home with him.

He was really looking forward to the arrival of his nieces in a couple of months, even felt a slight twinge of envy.

Where the hell had that come from?

He didn't want kids, did he?

No he assured himself, he was content with his life just the way it was for now. Having kids meant commitment and settling down and he was so not ready for that, maybe he never would be. He'd leave that to his sister and Mike he was happy for them, he really was, so why did his heart rate pick up speed at the thought of Kitty, glowing and pregnant with his child pop into his head. The thought of the vision coming true completely freaked him out.

Do I really want to settle down? He asked himself and shook his head at the absurdity of it. He enjoyed his single status, respectful, mutually beneficial no strings attached flings. He was happier that way, he bored easily once the challenge was over and he didn't want any messy complicated break ups, hurt feelings or recriminations. He just wanted to walk away without a backwards glance. There was still too much he wanted to achieve before he was ready to settle down.

But if that was true why couldn't he get her out of his head? Why did his heart rate pick up speed when he thought about her sensuous curves, satin soft golden skin, breathy sighs and feline, green eyes? Why did he get the feeling that this was it, this was why he'd been so restless lately, and this was what he'd been waiting for? Maybe he needed to re-evaluate pursuing her, then shook his head at the absurdity of his thoughts.

He was probably just coming down with something? yes that was it he assured himself, he was just a little stressed at the moment, thistemporary insanity would pass he was positive, it was just the whole new challenge thing that had him all fired up.

Happy with this conclusion he hugged and kissed his mother's cheek and slapped Greggs shoulder before taking his leave, promising to update them on the deal as it progressed. Gregg promised to do a little digging around and let him know what he came up with.

He got back in his car forcing his mind to formulate ideas about renovations as he made the 15 minute drive back to the office.

Chapter Eight

Kitty was dealing with a few enquiries as Blake rushed through the office and straight into his own, shutting his door without saying a word. He seemed pre-occupied and she nibbled on her bottom lip nervously as she worried about something being wrong. He must have changed his mind she thought and felt a moment's disappointment.

'Stop making mountains out of mole hills' Audrey snapped at her from her desk 'just because he didn't greet you with enthusiasm doesn't mean he's lost interest' she added 'you know how focused he can get when he's entering into a new deal, so just chill out for god sake' she said 'you're making me bloody nervous' she sighed

'Sure like that would ever happen' Kitty said dryly and berated herself under her breath. She needed to snap out this fixation she had on him. It was unhealthy and detrimental to her mental wellbeing, plus she didn't really have time for a fling, she assured herself. Then rolled her eyes at her own absurd behaviour.

'Kitty' Blake's voice sounded from his door 'do me a favour and get hold of Jake Masterson will you.

I'm on the phone to Len in legal but it won't take long, just give me 5 minutes before you put him through' then disappeared again behind his door. It seemed that there could be some kind of a problem with the deal after all and wracked her brains trying to figure out what it could be. Audrey snapped her fingers in front of her face to get her attention as she stood before her desk scowling down at her.

'Drink this and engage that brain of yours' she said dryly as she put down a coffee then moved towards Blake's door with another in hand.

Blake was in animated conversation with Len as Audrey walked in and put down his coffee and gave him her most disarming smile. He covered the mouth piece

'What are you plotting?' he asked her suspiciously and recoiled as she just grinned and left. God that woman was scary when she had something in her craw he thought, then became aware of Len's voice in his ear.

'Sorry Len, Audrey's just brought my coffee in, could you repeat that for me?' he asked and burst out laughing as Len bemoaned the fact that Blake's staff were so much more efficient than his.

He blew out a breath and had to bite back a retort about Audrey's armour plating and how Kitty had him tied in knots of sexual frustration, but thought better of it.

'Mavis is a little set in her ways' he admitted, she was over retirement age but had wanted to continue on for a few years.

She'd originally been with him but he'd replaced her with Audrey when she'd had extended time off due to a hip replacement. When she was fit again he'd placed her with Len as he worked at a more sedate pace. She was very old school, refused to call Len by his first name as it was disrespectful to his position. He also had to request refreshments as she didn't keep him in a regular supply.

'Set in her ways, I'm sure her contract was wrote on the tablet next to the 10 commandments' he groused and Blake grinned at the picture that represented. Okay, he admitted it, she was a little stiff and frail, going on 75 but she was an efficient sweetheart.

'Don't exaggerate you're just upset because I'm making you work at twice your normal speed on this one' and grinned at Len's indignant sputtering before he admitted.

'Fine, I concede, you owe me a game of squash for this one and I'll have everything ready for you by 10.30 tomorrow morning' he said as he ended the call. Blake sat back in his chair as the internal phone went.

'Jake Masterson for you on line 2' Kitty's velvet rasp snared around him, down the line, the hair on the back of his neck stood up and he snarled in frustration as other things stood up too.

'Thanks' he snapped with more vehemence than he'd intended but damn it, all it took was her voice to rouse his libido. He heard her huff just before the call connected.

'Jake I'm ringing with excellent news, I've got my legal department working on the contract as we speak' he informed him 'I believe your backer is Lance Edmonton? I'll sort out his payment personally for you so you no longer have to deal with him' he added relishing the thought of seeing Edmonton's face as he explained that he'd lost this round, scheming little weasel. His grin widened as Jake conceded.

'How about popping into the office in the morning around 11ish? We can get all the legalese out of the way, then I'll treat you to a celebratory lunch' he added and smiled warmly, at his immediate and relieved agreement. 'Enjoy the rest of your day Jake, I give you my personal assurance that I'll look after your hotel' he told him as he ended the call. He put the phone back into its cradle and leaned back leisurely in his chair, his hands behind his head, one foot resting on his knee as he stared at the ceiling in satisfaction.

He'd always wanted his own hotel, he was absolutely delighted that he'd just achieved his dream, well once it was all signed on the dotted line but that was just semantics. He was extremely excited about the coming venture and itching to get started.

He had visions of turning it from a drab, rather shabby tired building into an outstanding place of beauty. He could see it all so clearly now. He was going to have to shuffle some of his other work commitments around and do some delegating. He wanted in on the ground floor on this one, getting his hands dirty with the physical labour, he'd been stuck in an office too long and he needed to put his rusty learned skills to use, maybe that physical inactivity with his projects what was causing this restlessness in him he mused.

His architect was drawing up the new plans to his specifications, he'd run with Kitty's suggestions, they had merit and would add to the overall effect and use of the building, she had a good eye for detail.

It was going to take a lot of money and time to bring it up to the standard, so it still had to work as a viable means of income. The actual timetable still needed to be finalised around bookings etc., but he had faith in his contractors and employees. They'd get the job done with minimal disruption by either going floor to floor around room bookings or room by room if they had to. The dining wasn't too much of an issue they could move it to the conservatory area while the main dining room was overhauled. The kitchen was going to cause a slight problem, they'd have to close down for maybe a week to get that gutted and re-fitted but they'd worry about that once the ball was rolling properly.

The budget wasn't a problem either, a modernized apartment block had been completed at the beginning of the previous month and the majority had already sold. The last few had contracts going through at the moment so that gave him a decent dispersible cash flow to play with.

Everything was coming together and he was absolutely exhilarated, he felt like celebrating and he knew just the woman he wanted to do it with.

Kitty sat studiously hitting keys while she silently simmered, Blake had snapped at her for doing what he'd requested and putting Jake Masterson through to him. God she needed to get away from this tension riding her, right away from him, before she exploded again. She'd send her brother a text and invite him over for dinner. They could catch up and hit the cinema it had been ages since she'd done that and she really needed to feel on familiar ground. She felt like she was trying to sift her way through quick sand at the moment. Nothing was as it had been and she shuddered as ran her hands over her arms to ward off the chill that crept in.

While Audrey was on a post run on the floor below she pulled out her mobile and messaged Rob, he hit her back straight away

I'll pick you up outside at 5, dinner on me xx

She put her phone away and carried on opening up files on the latest apartments that were waiting on paperwork to complete the sales contracts. She either marked them as completed and attached any legal paperwork required or flagged them for further follow up.

She was happily humming, quietly under her breath now as she looked forward to her evening. It had been a couple of months since he'd been in the country and she'd been too busy to take any time off and visit him in Switzerland, where he was based.

'You're awfully chipper' Audrey commented suspiciously as she walked back in and sat down at her desk 'has something happened in the whole 10 minutes I've been out?'

'Yep, dinner with a very special man' she said with a wink, she was feeling happy and light-hearted and smug about getting one over Audrey. She'd actually left her speechless for a change as she tried desperately to figure out what she'd missed and hid a grin.

Kitty carried on ignoring the suspicious, speculative looks from Audrey now and again. She made sure she saved the work she'd finished and e-mailed Audrey all the relevant department information then backed it all up to the main file server, before she tidied her desk. She had 5 minutes before he arrive and didn't want to keep him waiting.

She disappeared into the bathroom with her handbag, removed her glasses and released her hair from the confining pins and sighed in pleasure as she gave it a thorough brushing. She swept on some tinted lip gloss and added some mascara for good measure. She frowned as she looked down at her dull, ill-fitting work clothes and sighed in resignation, she really wasn't dressed for anywhere up market, not that Rob would mind. As long as it was food he'd eat from a drive through and she smiled at the thought.

She loosened a couple of buttons on her blouse, left her jacket undone and stepped back from the mirror giving herself a quick once over. Satisfied she'd done all she could to make herself presentable she threw the discarded pins and glasses into her bag, turned and left.

Audrey's jaw dropped when she spotted Kitty leaving the toilet. Kitty ignored her shock at her transformation and grabbed her coat off the back of her chair, slinging it casually over her arm.

'See you in the morning' she waved cheerily as she got into the lift.

After a couple of seconds Audrey snapped out of her astonishment at what she'd seen and rapidly moved over to the window overlooking the entrance to the building, to get another look.

Blake walked out of his office and stood looking broodily at Kitty's empty chair and black screen. His head came up as he heard Audrey whistle and turned to see her upper body dangling out of an open window as she watched something below. He put his hands in his pockets and wandered over, his curiosity piqued and leaned over her shoulder to see what had her so fascinated.

His teeth clenched as he spotted Kitty far below, hair blowing in the early evening breeze and embracing a tall dark man before he helped her to slip into a silver Audi TT before getting into the driver's side and driving away.

'Well' Audrey whistled, as she pulled the window closed as the car got lost amongst the traffic, 'I wonder who that was?' only noticing Blake standing behind her as he put his hands out to steady her as she bumped into him. She turned to see the dark scowl on his face as he continued to glare out of the window. She grinned, she couldn't help it.

'Seems you have a little competition!' she added as she went over and cleared her own desk up, 'have a good evening' she called over her shoulder as she moved to the lift. She watched Blake rooted to the spot, hands jammed into his pockets and a face like thunder still glaring towards the window. Interesting, it seemed there was more to his interest in Kitty than even he realised.

Blake was absolutely livid, she'd blew him off for another man, him, no one ever blew him off, women adored him, what the hell had happened while he'd been closeted in his office? If she thought it was going to be easy to just write off what was between, then she was in for a very rude awakening.

He knew he was being illogical, he'd given her a choice in whether they pursued the chemistry between them. But to be honest, he'd never in a million years have thought that she'd turn him down. He was absolutely furious that she'd gone off with another man after the pleasure they'd shared this morning in his office, he felt like he'd been cuckolded. Kitty was his and he didn't share, not ever, they hadn't even scratched the surface yet and he'd be damned if he let her walk away before they'd thoroughly explored it from every angle.

He stormed back into his office and slammed the door his vision red with fury, he needed to calm down and think because obviously he needed to change his game plan. It seemed she was going to be even more of a challenge than he'd originally thought. Naïve of him he knew but he'd never had to work this hard for a woman before, ever and found he didn't much like it. His guts twisted as he visualized what could be happening between them even as he sat there. He slammed his fist down on his desk, he would not go there, and there was no way in hell she'd dive into bed with some other man after what had happened with them this morning. His angry haze lifted as he remembered the words she'd whispered in wonder. She'd told him she didn't like sex and he'd shown her how it could be if the right man was involved.

Well if you could call dry humping her sex he thought with disgust, not exactly a brilliant example of what they could have. To be fare though he'd been so close to the edge it was the only thing he'd been capable of. He groaned in despair as a thought occurred to him. Maybe now she'd had a taste of what she'd been missing she was eager to seek out what was on offer. Now that she'd had a taste and found that she like it, she would be like a kid let loose in a toy store, desperate to see all that was on offer. His earlier happy mood vanished in one quick flick of her hair as she'd disappeared inside another man's car.

He needed to get it together, he was not desperate, he assured himself, he could open up his little black book right now and have a woman in his bed within the hour, then winced as he ran an aggravated hand through his hair. The only problem with that particular scenario was that it just didn't appeal, not really. While it would feed the craving, the satisfaction would be fleeting and leave him feeling hollow and dissatisfied once the sheets cooled. He'd been there too many times over the last few years to count and it had left a bitter taste in his mouth. He just wasn't getting what he used to out of the fleeting relationships.

Kitty represented stimulation and a challenge, the first in a very long time, if ever. Now his appetite had been whetted he refused to give that up without a fight.

He could sit here all night mulling over all the different scenarios and outcomes for the coming project but to be honest it had lost some of its earlier sparkle, leaving him feeling somewhat deflated. Maybe he just needed to eat and have an early night, he'd probably feel much better in the morning and all these feelings of dissatisfaction and inadequacy would vanish with the appearance of a new day.

He turned his voicemail on and left.

Chapter Nine

Kitty sat in her front room, cross legged on the rug across from Rob, she'd changed into a pair of comfy slouchy pants and a baggy jumper as she was feeling a little chilled. She'd pulled her hair into a loose pony tail as soon as she'd got through the door. Rob had lost his tie, undone several buttons on his shirt and rolled his sleeves up as well as removing his socks and shoes. They had a "carpet picnic" as they'd called it when they were little, spread out between them before the fire. They'd decided on take away and a movie so they could kick back and relax.

Rob had stopped at a supermarket and picked up a copy of 'Taken 3', she'd not seen it yet and he'd assured her she'd enjoy it. Then they'd stopped at the local Chinese and ordered a banquet for two which they had spread out before them in various containers. They were just helping themselves to tastes of all the different dishes, a small glass of white wine each to accompany the meal, she'd found a small bottle at the back of her fridge.

She looked up at him as he groaned aloud after biting into a succulent piece of aromatic seasoned chicken breast and rolled her eyes.

'It's good to see you haven't changed' she grinned around a spring roll as she took an enthusiastic bite. He grinned back 'you neither, you still have the appetite of a sumo' and snorted with laughter, nearly choking himself in the process, as she childishly stuck her tongue out at him. They were close, but there again twins normally were. They looked very alike apart from eye colour, Rob had taken on their mother's golden ones a throw-back to her Persian ancestors and hers were green like their fathers. They'd been each other's companions and confidantes as they'd grown from children, watching each other's backs as they'd struggled to have some kind of a normal life.

It had been hard a couple of years ago because they'd both been suckered by a couple who'd realised who they were and had purposely set out to trap them. They could well have succeeded if not for her making an unscheduled visit to his flat one afternoon. She'd listened quietly in devastation to their discussion and had left shortly after to phone Rob to put him in the picture.

He at least hadn't been as stupid as to believe everything he'd been told, she on the other hand had been gullible and fallen hook line and sinker for the lies Nathan hold told to her. She'd even gone as far as to accept his marriage proposal thinking it was love. She'd left shortly after, doing her utmost to alter her appearance and start fresh far away from the scene of her disillusionment. She rolled her eyes at her own naivety and pushed the annoying thoughts away as they continued to work their way through the various dishes.

They cleared up and then Kitty sat on the floor curled up against the couch with a lightweight blanket over her cold legs. Rob lounged back on it, his feet up on the arm rest and his arms behind his head as they watched the film in companionable silence.

'Dad's coming over' he told her as the credits rolled and watched as her eyes widened in alarm as she turned to look at him resting her hands on the seat cushion. 'He's upset that you haven't been home in a while' he added 'He also wants to convince you to return to work at the hotel' he held his hand up 'hey don't shoot the messenger' he informed her with a grin as he watched the fire ignite behind her eyes. She was feistier than him and their father was in for a hell of a fight. It was always entertaining when the two clashed, Kitty had his stubborn streak, where he'd taken more after their mother, with a more sedate laid back nature.

'He's just worried about you' he said, giving her a sympathetic smile as he sat up and flung his legs down and he gave her shoulder a pat. He cleared his throat

'Mum doesn't know how much longer she can keep him on a leash' he added and Kitty laughed at that as he knew she would.

'Don't be absurd, she can wrap him around her little finger and you know it'. He grinned at her 'All it takes is a simper and a flutter of her lashes' she held her hand to her chest and fluttered her lashes to demonstrate and he guffawed at her antics, she did such a great impersonation of her. He knew what she meant though their dad might be a big powerful looking man that lots of people feared but he was an absolute pushover in the delicate little hands of their mother.

'I'm just warning you that he's going to turn up sooner rather than later' he said. He stretched and yawned, as the credits ended. 'I'm beat Kitten' he said, I think I'll head off, 'I've got a busy weekend ahead of me and I need to conserve my energy' he said with a teasing grin and she punched him in his knee, the only thing she could reach from her seat on the floor.

'You're despicable, your weekend probably consists of some poor besotted woman lavishing attention on your body' he gave her a wounded look but then spoiled it with the lascivious grin that eventually split his face.

'See, nothing important' and he rolled his eyes at her and mumbled under his breath

'I'm sure you can manage to crawl out of her bed for a few hours on Saturday evening' she joked, then burst out laughing as he stared at her with abject horror. 'Come on Rob, you can go back to your bedroom games afterwards, your genitalia intact' she made the sign of the cross over her heart in a silent promise. He cupped himself and winced not missing the threat of a swift knee to the groin that she was more than capable of delivering. He knew from experience how vicious she could be when riled.

He was pleased she'd got her fire back but was now curious as to who'd put it there? His musings ended as she smiled sweetly at him, never a good sign and he watched her warily 'It's in aid of the spinal injuries charity that Audrey's husband Dan runs. They'll receive 30% of all sales and commissions he receives' he looked thoughtfully at her and she could see him weakening. 'You know you'd feel bad if they didn't make a reasonable amount and the research folded' she added, turning the screw as she fluttered her lashes and he sighed in resignation, he knew when he was beat.

He was as pathetic as their father where his mother and Kitty were concerned, he thought with disgust.

'Okay, fine, e-mail me the details and I'll interrupt my precious leisure time to attend' he said with a pout, but his eyes were full of mirth. He pulled his shoes and suit jacket on, stuffing his socks and tie in the pocket as he grabbed his car keys up off the mantle.

Kitty walked him to his car, leaving the door open, her arm through his as she leaned her head against his chest. She missed these times and they'd gotten fewer as they'd gotten older. She stood on tip toe to kiss his cheek and ruffled his hair.

'Thank you for a great evening' she said with a grin, then squealed as he picked her up and gave her a tight squeeze.

'Sleep tight squirt, see you Saturday' he said as he put her back on her feet, tweaked her nose and got in his car.

She moved up the path and stood at the door rubbing her cold arms as she watched his car lights vanish around the corner. She tidied up, locked up, turned off the lights, picked up her blanket and made her way tiredly to bed.

She felt a lot more relaxed after her evening with Rob but was a little concerned about her father's imminent arrival; he could be tenacious when he got an idea in his head. There was nothing she could do about it now though and calling wouldn't put him off, so it was pointless obsessing over it, she'd have to deal with him when he arrived. She switched off the bedside lamp, pulled the duvet up around her shoulders and closed her eyes.

Sleep took her almost immediately but her dreams weren't pleasant, she didn't remember much just shadowy figures and anxiety. Consequently she woke feeling tired and grumpy her head was banging and felt like it was full of cotton wool. Her shower didn't help at all, maybe she was coming down with something, she thought as she sat slumped miserably on the bus on her way to work.

Chapter Ten

Blake had slept badly, so much for being energized after his early night, he'd tossed and turned for hours. His mind throwing out all sorts of erotic pictures of Kitty and entwined sweaty limbs and they didn't star him. He'd finally given in and got up to pace restlessly through his apartment feeling trapped and on edge. Around 3am he'd lost the plot completely and had gone to the basement car park and gotten into his car. He was going to drive by Kitty's flat, to see if the Audi was parked outside. Only the abject fear of what his obsession with her could mean to him and his single status had stopped him from actually following through. He'd been disgusted with his own behaviour, what the hell was the matter with him?

He'd finally crawled in bed bone weary and exhausted and had drifted off at around 4am to be woken at 6 by the smoke alarm going off in the apartment below. Idiot had burned his toast under the grill, he'd found out from Jerry the doorman as he'd headed to the gym on the first floor at 7am. He'd run off some of the weary tension in his body but was still tired and edgy when he stepped into his office at 8.15am.

Audrey was due in the next 15 minutes but he needed something to keep his hands and mind occupied so he set about filling up the drinks machine he'd installed in the corner of the outer office to replace the over used kettle. He'd just pressed for an extra strong coffee to wake himself up when the lift doors opened and Audrey walked in.

She dropped her bag on the floor beneath her desk and hung her coat on the back of her chair; he shook his head. Neither she nor Kitty used the coat stand that he'd purchased but stood empty in the corner near the toilets and wondered why he bothered. Thinking about Kitty made him scowl and Audrey placed her hands on her hips.

'I've not done a thing to warrant that look' she informed him, returning his scowl, then wandered over to the machine and pressed for her own cup of coffee. He waved away her response and she rolled her eyes at him as she lifted her now full doctored cup and took a sip as she made her way back to her desk.

'By the looks of you, you could do with a couple of those' she nodded towards his own cup as he raised it to his mouth frowning at her. 'Bad night?' she asked with a sickly sweet smile and he growled at her as he turned on his heel and went into his office. He heard her low laughter as he slammed the door shut with his foot in annoyance. At least someone was finding this whole sorry situation amusing, because he sure as hell wasn't.

He sat down and booted up his computer as he keyed in a couple of numbers and listened to his voice mail on speaker, while he continued to drink. He needed to get his head in the game. Jake would be here in a couple of hours to meet and sign the paperwork with himself, Len and Jeff; who was Mike's junior and was covering for him until he returned to work. He should be thrilled it was all coming together but this thing with Kitty had him tied up in knots, he seriously needed to let off some steam, then thought about Len's request for a game of squash. After he'd finished his celebratory lunch with Jake he'd see if Len wanted to take his offer up. Smashing a ball violently against a wall had immense appeal at the moment.

Kitty stepped out of the lift bleary eyed, flushed, yawning and shaking as she flung her coat behind her and flopped down in her seat. Audrey shook her head at her

'Someone else doesn't seem to have got much sleep?' she informed her as Kitty looked over at her miserably, her head felt like it was in a vice.

'I think I'm coming down with something' she said shakily, as she got up and made her way wearily over to the drinks machine. 'Do you want one?' she asked over her shoulder but Audrey refused. She put in an extra sugar to give her a boost and took her seat again noticing the way Audrey was watching her expectantly and sighed. She really wasn't in the mood to start answering questions, she'd deal with it tomorrow night when she felt a little better.

'I'm really not in the mood for explanations at the moment' she told her as she took a sip, cringing at the overly sweet brew.

'You seriously expect me to not ask?' Audrey sputtered. 'I watched you get in the car of a tall dark stranger and you honestly think I can keep quiet?' Kitty sighed in resignation.

'You'll meet him on Saturday, he's coming to the exhibition' she said and then sneezed loudly, she heard Audrey push back her chair and walk over. She closed her eyes and winced as her head began to thump painfully and felt a cool hand touch her forehead.

'Kitty, you're burning up' she tutted as she stepped back 'have you taken anything for it?' she said going back to her desk and rummaging through her bag as Kitty shook her head then winced as a sharp pain shot through the back of her head at the action. She slumped forward in her chair and rested her hot face against the cool desk and sighed. She felt absolutely dreadful, even worse now than when she'd woken up. Her whole body ached and she felt stiff and cold. A hand appeared in front of her face and she squinted up to see what she was being offered.

'Here, paracetamol and ibuprofen' Audrey informed her and waited while she sat up and dutifully popped the tablets into her mouth and swallowed them with a sip of her drink. 'You shouldn't have come in' she said as she sat on the corner of her desk and looked at her with concern. Dark circles marred her beautiful face and her eyes were glazed with fever. She got up as Kitty leaned forward again to rest her hot face back on her desk.

'I'll be fine in a minute' she muttered and then her teeth started to chatter as she was wracked with chills.

Audrey had seen enough, the girl was sick and she was being thick headed and stubborn. She wasn't doing herself any favours by trying to carry on, she got up and went over and knocked on Blake's door.

Blake was reading through the files on the upcoming meeting, it was the most expensive piece of property he'd purchased to date. Although the figures were high, he knew in his gut that it was a worthwhile investment. He dialled Jeff in accounts to check that his estimations for renovations were realistic, listening intently to his responses.

They talked over speaker phone to make it easier as they both flicked through screens and files but he stopped mid-sentence as Audrey stepped into his office after a quiet tap.

She looked a little panicky, wringing her hands and biting her lip and he grew concerned, Audrey was not a worrier, something must be seriously wrong if it had her ruffled.

'Can I ring you back Jeff? Audrey needs to speak to me' he informed him

'Sure' he replied and the call disconnected. He got up from his desk and moved cautiously towards her.

'What's wrong, you look worried?' he said as he stood in front of her studying the lines of worry and indecision etched into her brow.

'It's Kitty' she whispered looking over her shoulder in anxiety and his heart banged painfully against his ribs as he felt his stomach turn over in fear.

'What's wrong with Kitty?' he asked his own imagination running wild, thoughts flew through his mind about her lying injured somewhere after being in an accident. His gut twisted painfully at the thought of her being hurt, or worse. His concern must have shown because she grabbed onto his arm and pushed him away from the door and further into his office.

'She's fine' she said and then shook her head 'no she's not fine' she said her hand fluttering around and he frowned at her as he tried to make sense out of what she was talking about, his temper snapped in his agitation

'Either she's fine or she isn't, which is it?'

'Shush' she told him and he looked at her incredulously 'She's lying over her desk, burning up, shivering and her eyes are glazed with fever, she shouldn't be here' she told him with annoyance as if it was his fault. He'd heard enough as he stepped around her and made his way into the outer office to check for himself.

She looked forlorn and utterly miserable as she lay with her face resting on top of her desk. She was flushed and her eyes were screwed tightly closed as if in pain and his heart twisted in his chest. He knelt down beside her and put his hand against her forehead and winced at the heat he encountered. Her eyes flickered open at the contact and he noticed that they were indeed glazed and not in a good way. They also didn't seem to be focusing properly and he looked over his shoulder towards Audrey as she came up anxiously behind him.

'I've given her a couple of paracetamol and an Ibuprofen' she said 'she really needs to go home but I don't drive and Kitty comes in on the bus' she added and bit her lip.

'Should I call a taxi for her?' and he shook his head, grabbed her coat and bag and scooped her off the chair and into his arms. Her head lay limply against his shoulder and her body went floppy, he went rigid with panic, his heart seemed to stop in his chest as he held his breath, then he felt her shiver and he relaxed again taking a deep breath as his heart rate began to beat out a normal rhythm.

He could feel the heat off her body through his clothes and it made him uncomfortably warm in all the places they touched. God knows how bad she felt, he needed to get her out of here and bring down her temperature quickly. He stopped dead in his tracks as it hit him. Her health and welfare were more important to him at the moment than finalizing a crucial deal, it had never happened before. He should have felt some trepidation over this overwhelming need he had to see to her care personally but didn't. It felt right, she fit in his arms and oddly enough he liked her being there, he wasn't the least concerned about it. She was now his top priority, everything else could be handled by someone else and he needed to delegate quickly so he could get her home.

'Call Jeff back in accounts will you and tell him I'm leaving it to him to sort out Jake Masterson when he arrives' he did a quick mental inventory 'tell him to give my apologies to Jake and explain that something important came up unexpectedly and I needed to leave'. He watched in fascination as Audrey's eyebrows rose further and further up her forehead as he spoke. 'Tell him to let Jake know that I'll ring him myself later to answer any concerns he has once I've sorted it out. Meaning I have Kitty settled of course, but no one needs to know that' he added, looking at her meaningfully. Then headed towards the lift but stopped mid step and turned back. 'Damn, nearly forgot my keys, they're in my jacket pocket, can you just grab it off my chair for me?' he asked as Audrey turned tail and ran into his office coming back out with it over her arm. 'Oh can you also give Len a ring and tell him to bring Alison with him to the meeting, she'll need to take notes; she's more than capable'. He watched Audrey's mouth compress with annoyance and sighed, Alison was training to take over from Mavis once she retired, but she was capable and trustworthy. It seemed he'd upset Audrey unintentionally, he hadn't meant to. He ran his spare hand through his hair in agitation and looked at her as her eyes flashed with annoyance and her mouth opened to berate him. He didn't give her a chance, he spoke first and took the wind out of her sales.

'You're going to be holding the fort down here for me' he said 'which I really appreciate and I trust you implicitly. You're unflappable and I can rely on you in a crisis to keep a clear head' he added with a slight tilt to his lips. He was relieved to see her face calm instantly and her eyes light up with warmth. He turned away and pressed the call button on the lift, the doors opening for him instantly and he stepped inside and leaned against the back rail as it began its descent, Kitty tucked against him.

He ignored the interested looks he got as he left the lift in the underground parking lot and headed towards his car. He juggled her around so he could reach into his jacket pocket and pull out his keys. Once he hit the fob he had to balance her bottom on his knee so he could open the door, luckily for him he kept in shape and she wasn't heavy. He placed her carefully on the passenger seat and strapped her in, then quickly ran around and jumped in the driver's side. Slinging his jacket and her coat and her bag on the back seat as he shut the door and started the engine. He turned the volume down on the radio as it burst to life, hoping it hadn't disturbed her and looked over to see that her eyes were still closed. She seemed to be sleeping fitfully, her head lolling on her chest, several strands of her hair had escaped their confinement and were sticking to her damp skin and he itched to rub it between his fingers so he could feel its texture.

Rush hour traffic added an extra 15 minutes to what should have been a fairly quick trip, she only lived 8 miles away from the office.

He pulled up outside her flat and switched off the engine and leaned over the seats to find her keys in her bag. Well he hoped that was where they were? That's where she'd dropped them when he'd taken her to dinner the other night. He rummaged around for a while before he felt the tell-tale cold hard feel of them and pulled them into his hand. He got out and moved around to retrieve her from the passenger seat.

She was still sleeping as he slipped quietly into her flat and toed the door closed behind him. He carried her down the hallway, opening the first door on the right; the one he'd seen her disappear into when he'd picked her up. He couldn't miss the bed it was a huge four poster affair, pushed against the back wall. His took in the romantic setting and smiled, she really did hide her sensuous side well but it was blinding obviously in her bedroom décor. Her bed was covered in deep purple gauzy voile held back with twisted gold rope and her bedding was silk, the same shade of purple with swirling gold patterns.

Scatter cushions were piled on top in differing shades of purple, gold and cream. Her carpet was cream and the walls looked like they were made from cream, purple and gold marble.

He knocked the scatter cushions to the floor and pulled back the duvet as he placed her on the cream cotton bottom sheet. Then stood back undecided what to do about her clothes, if her left her in them she was going to be uncomfortable. They really needed to go to help bring down her temperature, the less she wore the quicker it would drop.

He took a deep fortifying breath and leaned over her, trying to be circumspect as he removed her skirt suit and blouse. He tried not to stare at her lacy baby pink matching underwear and black hold up stockings but failed miserably, he was only a man. He pulled off her clunky shoes with distaste and rolled down her stockings before pulling them off her feet, and grinned as he spotted her pink toe nails. She was a mass of contraction and she fascinated him. She was all sensual heat and fire under her dower exterior. He folded her clothes and placed them on the bedding box at the end of the bed. He averted his eyes once he had her down to her underwear, refusing to acknowledge all the curves and expanse of honey toned smooth skin that was revealed. He took a moment to look around and get his bearings.

French windows to the left hung with gauzy flowing cream Voile and full length vertical blinds. He went over and closed the blinds to block out the weak autumn sun and spotted a door that was slightly ajar. He moved towards it and peeped inside, relieved to see that it was a walk in wardrobe and walked in and grabbed the first t-shirt his hand landed on and left. He knelt on the bed to pull it over her head and jiggled her around as gently as he could to put her arms through and quickly pulled it down over her torso, relieved that it stopped mid-thigh. He stood back up unsure of what to do next when his eyes lit on the big bold print emblazoned across the front and stared open mouthed.

'GET IT WHILE IT'S HOT', was emblazoned between two steaming buns, across her ample breasts. He stamped down on the completely inappropriate thoughts that started to take flight and averted his eyes once again. A gilt and material armed chair was in the corner and a lightweight blanket was flung carelessly over it. He pulled it off, carried it back and covered her quickly, not comfortable with the expanse of thigh still on show.

He sighed with relief now that he had her settled in her bed but scowled as he notice most of her hair was still confined in that god awful style she insisted on for the office. Surely that would add to the discomfort she must already have in her aching head. He quickly felt around and pulled all the pins out dropping them on the white wood bedside table refusing to look at her long black hair flowing over the pillows.

He still needed to bring her temperature down, her bedroom was rather warm "or was that him" he thought cynically with a twist of his mouth. An oscillating fan stood in the opposite corner so he moved it closer to the bed, put it on a low stationary setting and pointed it above her, he didn't want it blowing directly onto her he just wanted to cool her down, not give her a chill.

Deciding that he'd done everything he could for the moment he left the bedroom and went looking for the kitchen. She needed some fluids in her system before she de-hydrated because of the heat her body was producing. He was relieved when he found the kitchen through the living room. It was clean and bright, white walls and units, with stainless steel appliances and a shiny black work surface. He found a tall glass on the draining board and when he opened her fridge a large bottle of still water was in the door shelf. He filled up the glass, put the bottle back and padded back into her bedroom. She hadn't moved from where he'd placed her but the shaking seemed to have lessened.

He put his arm under her neck to help lift her head and put the glass to her mouth, relieved when her lips parted automatically and she obligingly swallowed half the glass. She sighed as he placed her head back on the pillow and he stood staring down at her for a moment, then gave himself a shake placed the half full glass down on her bedside cabinet and felt her forehead again. Some of the heat had gone but she was still flushed. Her breathing seemed more natural now, less laboured and smiled as she sighed again then rolled onto her side and placed a hand under her cheek. Assured he'd done everything he could and she was comfortable for now, he bent down and placed a kiss on the top of her head and heard her mumble sleepily. He stepped back, so as not to disturb her further, he was a little uncomfortable at how much she affected him.

He was still staggered that he'd never registered in the last 2 years how extraordinarily beautiful she was. He must have been walking around with blinkers on he thought as he left the room, leaving the door ajar, so he'd hear her.

He needed his jacket from the car as his mobile was in his pocket and he'd also left Kitty's jacket and bag there. He quietly slipped out leaving the door ajar and quickly retrieved the items. He shut the door and moved into her living room to make the call to Jake.

He sat listening to the ring tone as he spotted the photographs again on her mantle and moved over to take a closer look when a voicemail kicked in. He left a quick message to give his apologies and a promise to ring him later. He slipped his phone into his trouser pocket and picked the first photograph up to take a closer look. It was of a younger more carefree Kitty, she was stood beside a tall young man his hair the same shade of midnight black as hers. Their eyes were different colours though, although on further inspection he noticed that they had same tilted shape and wondered if he was a relative.

He scoffed at that, what he meant was he hoped he was a relative because they looked happy and comfortable with each other. He was also positive this was the man she'd left work with yesterday. He scowled at the thought and put it back, picking up the 2nd one.

This was of an older couple, the man extremely broad, his hair jet black with silver flecks here and there but his eyes were the same shade of green as Kitty's, no not quite the same he saw on closer inspection. They were a different shape and there was something else different about the colour that he couldn't quite put his finger on. The petite golden haired woman tucked under his wide shoulder had the same shaped eyes as hers but they were an unusual golden colour like the flecks in Kitty's eyes. He picked up the first picture again and studied the younger man more closely this time.

He was relieved to find that his eyes were the exact same shade of gold and his face split in a huge grin.

'Sneaky' he said grudgingly, this had be her brother and the other picture that of her parents but something was niggling him, the older couple looked familiar to him but he couldn't remember from where? Was it something he'd seen on the news or was it from an article he'd read? He was trying desperately to jog his memory, frustration running through him when he heard retching coming from nearby. He let the memory go, it would come eventually and placed the pictures back on the mantle as he went to investigate.

Kitty felt terrible, her head was banging and as she opened her eyes the room was spinning, her stomach cramped with nausea pains, she managed to sit up then frowned as she found herself in her bed. She didn't remember coming home? She was home though wasn't she? She took a deep breath to try and alleviate the pain she knew the action would cause as she looked up above her. She relaxed as she found her familiar gathered material above her head, it was her own bed she thought and slumped back. Then she noticed that she was wearing one of her old night shirts, one of the innuendo ones that Rob liked to buy her because they amused his weird sense of humour. She just managed to stop herself from rolling her eyes, knowing it would hurt like a son of a bitch. Who had undressed her? Then she let the confusing thoughts go as the stomach cramps intensified. Her mouth started to water and she vaulted out of bed. She needed to be sick but she crumpled to the floor as she stumbled over the scatter cushions spread around the floor, the motion making the room spin alarmingly. She grabbed onto the bedside cabinet to steady herself and then thought better of it and dropped down onto her hands and knees to crawl to the bathroom next door. She'd just managed to lift the toilet seat as her stomach emptied violently and she lay her head weakly against the side of the bowl as it was over.

Sweat was covering her body as she shivered with cold, then shuddered with the after effects of her stomach emptying.

She heard someone enter behind her but didn't have the energy to lift her head. She didn't even care if she was going to be robbed or murdered at present, she felt too dreadful to care. She was spent and completely weary but at least her stomach no longer felt cramped.

Blake found her on the bathroom floor, her forehead pressed against the toilet bowl as her body shook. He moved forward cautiously not wanting to frighten her.

'Hey, need a hand?' he asked as he knelt down beside her, brushing his hand through her damp hair and pushing it out of the way so he could see her face. He was glad to see that her eyes had lost the glaze of fever but they still looked slightly unfocused, she was also ghostly pale. Her forehead was beaded with sweat and her usually berry coloured lips looked grey.

She squinted up at him forlornly, and he felt a weird shifting sensation in his chest as he took in her still beautiful, but very ill features. She hadn't even bothered to berate him about being in her home, "she must really feel like crap" he thought with concern. He turned the tap on in the sink and wet a facecloth that was folded on top of the hand towel on a heated rail. He rung out the worst of the moisture and ran it over her face and lifted her hair and did the same to the back of her neck and heard her sigh.

'Come on, you need to get back in bed' he said as he put the cloth in the sink and gently put his hands under her legs and lifted her into his arms again. Her head slumped onto his shoulder and she relaxed against him, one hand lightly holding onto the back of his neck as he took her back to her room. He placed her back on her bed and pulled the lightweight cover up over her again. He offered her a drink of the water to help swill the taste away and was relieved to see that she had the energy to lift her own head as she sipped thirstily, emptying the rest of the glass. She lay back down and her eyes closed on a shaky sigh. He'd just turned to leave when he heard her say

'Thanks Blake, I know you must have brought me home and taken care of me, I do appreciate it' she said her voice no louder than a croaky whisper.

'Anytime' he said as he turned and left the room her breathing already evened out as she slipped back to sleep.

He went back into the bathroom, dropped the toilet seat, flushed away the evidence of her illness, then rinsed out the wash cloth and placed it back on the heated towel rail.

He looked around him for the first time, the bathroom was as clean and fresh as the kitchen. A white suite and tiled floor with chrome Knick knacks, which matched the shower head over the rolled top bath. A cream marbled effect shower curtain hung from a chrome rail and the colour was a perfect match to the rest of the tiles that went from floor to ceiling. Vertical blinds at the small window with what he now considered her signature voile hung from either side. The colour in here was mocha and it matched the vein in the marbling precisely. Someone had a great eye for detail, her flat might be small compared to his apartment but it was decorated with an expert attention to detail.

He'd have to ask her who her decorator was when she was feeling better, he wouldn't mind bringing them on board in the refurbishment of the hotel. He smacked himself in the head as he remembered the closure meeting that was probably well under way by now. He pulled his phone from his pocket to ring Audrey and listened to the dial tone as he took the glass back to the kitchen for a refill.

He leaned against the sink staring through the window at her small back yard. It had a decked area with a small wrought iron table and chairs. A swing chair stood under a wooden arch that was covered in green ivy, the rest of the yard gravelled with strategically placed flower urns. In the corner a small statue of Venus stood pouring water into a larger urn.

'Is everything alright Blake?' he heard in his ear as she answered the phone and turned his back on the view to concentrate on the call. After giving her an update on Kitty's health he asked a few questions of his own and listened with satisfaction as he was informed that everything was fine, running like clockwork in fact and that she'd booked a table for lunch for them afterwards, he had nothing to worry about. He disconnected after thanking her and put his phone away.

Just as he switched the kettle to make himself a drink his restless night finally caught up, a huge yawn stretched his jaw painfully and made his eyes water. He passed on the drink, what he really needed was forty winks.

He left the kitchen and tiptoed tiredly back towards Kitty's room to check on her. Finding her once again curled on her side with her hand under her cheek and sleeping peacefully. He left the fresh glass of water on the bedside table and went back to her living room, lowering himself into the large comfortable looking chair. He groaned in pleasure as he was cocooned in comfort, like sinking into feathers. Rubbing at his eyes, they were gritty with lack of sleep, his lids heavy as he fought to keep them open, he assured himself that Kitty was fine for now. He yawned again as they slid closed on the thought that if she woke up and needed anything he'd hear her, as he finally succumbed to the sleep his body desperately craved.

Kitty came awake slowly, her head wasn't as spacey now and a lot of the ache in her body had disappeared, she turned over and squinted at the bedside clock and groaned. It was 2.30pm she must have been out for hours. She had a foggy recollection of Blake wiping her brow and tucking her back into bed. Surely that wasn't right, she must have been hallucinating due to the fever. He just didn't seem the type to be comfortable around ill people, he was always so disgustingly healthy and active. She wouldn't be surprised if he had an engine instead of a heart, the man was a machine. He was constantly on the go at work or with a beauty on his arm, socializing and networking at glittering functions of the rich and famous. When he wasn't doing that he was down the gym working out or running.

She pushed the cover off and gingerly sat up, swinging her legs onto the floor and noticed that there was no sound in the apartment, no movement at all. She must have been hallucinating earlier and shrugged her shoulders as she took a steadying breath and pushed herself upright. She closed her eyes for a second while she adjusted to the new position then tentatively made her way to the bathroom. She needed more paracetamol but she'd have to remember that she seemed to have an adverse reaction to ibuprofen. That was the only thing she had never taken before and could put down to the bout of stomach cramp and vomiting.

She opened the medicine cabinet in the bathroom and pulled down her preferred pain relief and popped two in her mouth and cupped her hand under the running water in the sink and swallowed. She shut the door and caught a glimpse of her tangled hair, dull eyes and pale blotchy face in the mirror and groaned at the sight. Then shrugged it off, she wasn't out to impress anyone, which was a good job because she still felt rough as hell and she looked a mess.

She had a disgusting taste in her mouth, her tongue felt fury and her mouth was dry. She grabbed her tooth brush and brushed her teeth and tongue, to remove the horrible taste and freshen up her breath.

She lifted the lid in the toilet relieved that the earlier crime scene it had resembled had vanished and sighed as she sat down and took care of business. Her stomach gave a loud growl, cramping with emptiness this time. She washed her hands in the sink and flushed the chain. Food, she needed food and some fresh orange, she salivated at the thought and made her way to the kitchen.

As she stepped into the living room she noticed a sleeping form in her chair. She blinked to try and clear her vision but no, still there and on closer inspection she saw that it was Blake. Not the hallucination she'd thought him earlier and moved closer to get a better look.

He was slumped down, legs out in front of him with his feet crossed at the ankles and his arms folded and hands tucked under his arms. His head hung down onto his chest in what looked to be a really uncomfortable position. His hair was messed up and his 5 o'clock shadow looked darker than she'd ever seen it, she frowned as she watched him twitch in his sleep.

Why had he taken care of her?
And more to the point why was he still here?
His caring actions went against all the things she thought she knew about him, well unless he was hoping to gain brownie points in the seduction game. She snorted at her own thoughts, he didn't look much better than her at the moment, although he wasn't pale. He did have dark circles under his eyes and had to dig her short nails into her palms to stop herself from leaning over and brushing his hair back off his forehead. He looked innocent and vulnerable in sleep, and shook her head, where the hell had that thought come from, Blake, innocent and vulnerable did not belong in the same sentence. Maybe she was more ill than she'd thought or maybe she was still sleeping? That thought vanished as her hunger made itself known again with another loud growl.

She dropped her thoughts and worries about Blake and tip toed passed him into the kitchen in search of sustenance and that orange juice as her stomach made yet another noisy protest.

She had her head in the fridge rummaging for something quick to heat up, her eyes and hands moving things about as she made her way through the shelves. As her eyes dropped to the eggs on the bottom shelf she became aware of no longer being alone, as from her vantage point a large pair of black brogues appeared behind her.

Blake was woken suddenly when his phone vibrated in his trouser pocket. He unfolded his arms and pulled it out to look at the message on screen.

'Deal all signed, out now having celebratory lunch!!'

he read with satisfaction, then slipped it back as he turned his stiff neck from side to side to relieve it, ran his hand down his tired face and pushed his hair out of his eyes with annoyance before hoisting himself up from the chair. He walked quietly towards the kitchen to investigate a noise he'd heard coming from there, but stopped at the open doorway and grinned appreciatively at the view.

Kitty was bent over double, her head inside the fridge as she moved things around and muttered to herself. His grin widened as he took in the fascinating display of her barely covered rounded bottom stuck up in the air and his interest piqued as it moved invitingly from side to side in response to her rifling motions. The t shirt he'd put on her had risen giving him a spectacular view of her tiny pink panties and he felt his libido kick in as he moved forward.

She suddenly stopped moving, she must have noticed his feet he realised as he looked down and spotted her hair trailing along the floor near her own bare feet. She slowly pulled her head out and straightened as she turned slowly to face him.

His libido died as he took in how pale she still was and the dark smudges marring her usually healthy glowing skin, placing the back of his hand against her forehead he checked to make sure that her temperature had cooled. He scowled at her as he started to have inappropriate thoughts about her, well inappropriate as she wasn't well, he thought with disgust. He was overly conscious of the length of bare smooth leg on show and was annoyed that he couldn't control his reaction to her.

What the hell did she have that no one else did? He still hadn't figured that one out and he hated not being able to solve puzzles. Maybe that was why he was so interested in her, the thought soothed his ego, but he nearly snorted at the bald lie. He needed to remove the temptation she was, especially the way she was dressed or undressed as may be. He bent down and picked her up with the intention of putting her back to bed and out of his reach. If she was hungry he'd make her something, he just needed a little distance to regain some self-control.

Kitty was horrified as she realised how little she was wearing, she'd known of course on a subconscious level but the circumstances hadn't really registered. She hadn't known he was really there, she'd thought he was a hallucination. She was mortified as he picked her up and she felt the heat hit the back of her thighs and felt the hairs on his naked forearms set tingles off as he held her securely against his hard frame. She bit her lip to hold back a groan at the sensation.

It was her own fault she was in this position she reminded herself, if she'd just put on a dressing gown before venturing out she wouldn't have been caught half naked, she thought with mortification.

Then her anger surfaced as she remembered that this was her home, she lived here alone, she should be able to stride around half naked, or fully for that matter, if that's what she was inclined to do. He was trespassing but her mind shied away from that thought, he'd gone out of his way to take care of her when she had been incapable. Something stirred in the back of her mind and she grabbed onto his shoulder as he moved her back into her bedroom and placed her back on her bed and covered her up, then turned to leave again.

'The meeting .... did you miss your meeting?' she asked

'Yes, but the deal is done, Jeff and Len took over for me and I received a confirmation text a little while ago, that's what woke me up' he said and heard her shocked gasp and sighed as he turned back to her.

Was he really that bad, that much of a workaholic? Probably he conceded but he was going to make more of a concerted effort to relax he decided as he looked over at her. He couldn't remember the last time he'd taken a break, a real break away from business and all its demands. Kitty getting ill had brought home to him how quickly life could change but why her? Mike and Melanie's situation should have shown him that? He was confused. His small family was precious to him, they were his world, the reason he'd fought so hard to get where he was. But at what personal cost? And why was it only now bothering him?

He looked pointedly at her

'You have to learn who to and when to delegate, that's just good business sense' he added and as he left and heard her sputter indignantly. He grinned at her annoyance with him, it was a good sign that she was on the mend.

He made his way into the kitchen, thoughts and indecision playing on his mind, how many years had he wasted, well not wasted exactly he just hadn't really stopped to take stock of what he could possibly be missing out on. He'd plodded on oblivious to other people, he had become selfish he realised as he had carried on building his fortune and business connections, and it was a rather sobering thought.

He let his personal introspection go, now wasn't the time, Kitty needed food. He pulled out the fixings for an omelette and routed through the cupboards to find a frying pan. Once he'd added some mushrooms and peppers to the bubbling mix and added some seasoning, he popped a couple of rounds of bread in the toaster and flicked the kettle on to make a warm drink for himself.

Chapter Eleven

Kitty sat up in bed and silently fumed, he'd put her back here like a naughty child. She was feeling much better and desperately needed something to eat, she was starving. Indecision battled with her conscience, she knew he thought he was doing what was best for her, high handed of him, but sweet none the less. The only problem was that her stomach was beginning to ache with hunger pangs, she needed food. She'd just swung her legs off the bed in an attempt to try again, when the delicious aroma of cooking food wound its way into her bedroom. She sniffed appreciatively and licked her lips as she dragged her feet back onto the bed and shoved her pillows up into a more comfortable sitting position.

Blake appeared again, this time carrying a tray. He put it down across her knees

'Eat' he said gruffly, then turned and left, not even giving her a chance to respond or thank him. She ignored his foul mood, too hungry to care and looked down to see what he'd brought her? She found a plate filled with a succulent looking omelette, some lightly buttered toast and a glass of ice cold fresh orange juice and sighed as she breathed in the tantalising aromas. Picking up the fork she tucked in ravenously, the omelette was so light and fluffy it practically melted in her mouth. The wonderful flavour burst on her tongue, suffusing her with the heady taste of the creamy egg and milk, bitter green pepper and slightly salty mushroom, he'd added. She groaned appreciatively and cleared her plate within minutes, so hungry she'd basically inhaled. She sat back replete now the stomach cramps had gone and frowned as she admitted grudgingly that she'd have to add yet another thing to the growing list of his talents. He seemed to excel at everything he set his mind to.

The man oozed confidence, was gorgeous, intelligent, good company, could cook and had shown her a caring side she wouldn't have believed possible, had she not seen it first-hand. She'd always thought him a little remote and unfeeling, moving from woman to woman without a care, but maybe he didn't see it that way, she knew Rob didn't. A relationship with him seemed more appealing the more she got to know him. He'd definitely grown on her and to be honest she was tired of fighting this attraction between them.

The only downside to it was he seemed to be a complete commitment phoebe and that worried her greatly. He would be so easy to fall for and although her last couple of relationships had hurt her pride, she was positive with him, much more than her pride would be shattered if it went wrong. She nibbled thoughtfully on a piece of toast as she considered the dilemma she was in. Her body was definitely on board with the idea but her heart and mind were in conflict.

She knew that while they were compatible physically, well that was an understatement, they were combustible! They also had similar tastes in literature and films but there was still so much she didn't know about him. There was also a lot he didn't know about her she thought and frowned as an unpalatable thought struck. Maybe he didn't want to know? After all he hadn't asked, maybe all he wanted was access to her body and she bit her lip in indecision. If that was the case she knew she'd be devastated, that once again her taste in men was lousy. She wasn't sure if she was ready to settle down but she was adult enough to admit that she did want to explore this thing between them. What was she going to do if all he wanted was a temporary physical relationship with her? Would she really have the strength to walk away? She wasn't sure, then snorted at her own lie. If she was completely honest, she thought he was worth the risk. He had something the other men hadn't and that was integrity, he was a wealthy successful business man and he couldn't possibly he using her to make money, he already had enough of his own, surely?

It seemed she'd made her decision, she just needed to tell him and found herself panicking at the idea, how was she supposed to bring it up? Or was she just meant to seduce him? Although she found the idea appealing, she didn't really have a clue how to go about it, she'd never had to or wanted to; before now that is. She'd need to do some research and knew just where to go for it, her brother dated a lot too, he'd know what sort of things turned a man on and he'd tell her. She smiled with relief her decision now made, she'd covered all the angles and was going in with her eyes wide open. She just hoped to god she didn't live to regret it and end up with her heart irrevocably broken.

She snuggled back into the pillows and found her eyes drooping, how on earth could she still be tired? She'd already slept most of the day away she thought fuzzily as she yawned and her eyes drifted closed.

Blake forced himself back into the kitchen and sat down at the small table to eat alone, specifically because what he really wanted, was to sit down and talk with Kitty awhile. He wanted to get to know her better, to see her smile but that had set off alarm bells in his head. The intimacy of her room wasn't conducive to friendly chatter and now he was no longer worried about her health he needed to put his feelings into perspective.

Although he found her intriguing and knew he would enjoy the challenge of seducing her, he was no longer sure he wanted to go down that route. He knew instinctively that that way would lead to disaster. Although he knew something was missing from his life and that's why he'd become bored of his affairs, he really didn't know if he was ready to, or capable of having a long term relationship?

He didn't know what the hell he wanted, well apart from Kitty but he wasn't sure if spending time with her was the answer. He knew he'd enjoyed her intelligence as well as her body but he was concerned her emotions would become involved. Who was he kidding, so were his and that would lead to unhappiness on both sides if things went wrong.

Kitty had forever written all over her and he could admit to being a coward, he didn't know if he was capable of giving her what she needed? He'd never tried.

He was a mass of contradictions at the moment, she was so far removed from what he normally went for; on every level, that he then wondered if that's what he found most attractive about her? He knew they'd be good together, but would it be enough or was he just overcomplicating things?

Maybe he just needed to stop thinking all together and just see what happened. He brightened at the thought, he could take things slowly, feel his way through. He was strong enough to protect himself and her from hurt, he was sure and they could have some fun getting to know each other. He thought too much he knew, he over analysed he thought, then laughed at his own confusion. What the hell was the matter with him? He was never usually this indecisive when it came to women. He usually just took what was on offer and didn't worry about the consequences, so what was so different this time? He shrugged his shoulders in irritation and finished his toast, he was doing it again, over analysing, treating this as he did a business venture, but that couldn't be transferred to this particular problem. With people there were too many variables.

He was going to listen to his first thoughts and take some time, he was going to relax and have some fun with Kitty, live a little, enjoy some time away from the business and see where it lead. He'd damn well earned it.

That settled he got up and loaded his dishes into the integrated dishwasher he'd located to the side of the sink, then went back to check on Kitty. He wanted to see if she'd managed to eat anything?

As he stepped into her room he saw that she'd fallen asleep again, snuggled back into her pillows, the tray balanced precariously on her lap with the empty dishes on it. He felt a smile tug at his lips as he tip-toed over; so as not to disturb her. He very gently leaned forward and with one hand gripped the tray, before he could remove it he was startled by an electric sensation that shot up his arm, as his hand accidentally brushed along hers. He pulled his hand back quickly and gave it a shake to shift the sensation, then gritting his teeth he changed position and this time successfully managed to remove it without any contact. He moved back, tray in hand and took in the hair flowing over her pillow and the fan of black lashes on her cheeks. He was pleased to see that her normal colour had returned and that her sleep was much more natural now, not fever induced. He watched as her mouth parted slightly as she took her next breath, her lashed fluttered as she began to stir. He should leave, while he still had the sense to keep his hands to himself.

The next time she woke she should be stronger and more able to care for herself leaving him free to leave. He frowned at the thought, he'd become rather fond of her little flat, it was much more comfortable and inviting than his own aesthetically pleasing apartment. Everything he had, had been chosen specifically because it was expensive and looked the part of a wealthy business man, not because it was particularly comfortable or even to his own tastes. The only comfortable piece he owned was his bed, which he always slept in alone. His affairs were carried out in the women's homes or on neutral territory and he never spent the night. That would bring intimacy into his relations and that wasn't what they were about. If he brought a woman into his personal space it would give off the wrong impression. He had fleeting affairs to assuage his sexual appetites, nothing more. He may wrap it up by supplying conversation, compliments and expensive meals and gifts but it was not true intimacy. He only wrapped it up in civilized veneer to soothe his own conscience, nothing more. He was staggered at how much he'd changed and he wasn't at all sure if he liked who he'd become.

What he really hungered for was a sense of home, like the feeling he got when he sat in his mums inviting kitchen or the rather comfortable chair that he'd napped in earlier. He couldn't imagine falling asleep on the upright bucket seat that he had or the modern black leather sofa that matched it. He really needed to change his ways, especially his home environment. He'd now had a taste of feeling truly comfortable and relaxed in his surroundings and was ashamed to say that he'd forgotten how that had really felt, until now.

Kitty became aware of no longer being alone, she watched Blake through her lashes as he stood watching her from the side of her bed. He seemed to be deep in thought, his brow furrowed as if he was trying to work out a particularly difficult problem. She again had the absurd feeling of wanting to touch him but this time to comfort him.

This was bad, she just knew that she was going to get badly burned this time, if she wasn't very careful.
She must have done something to alert him to the fact that she'd woken because his brow cleared and she watched in fascination as his features smoothed out. He produced a nice facsimile of a smile, that didn't quite reach his eyes. She would play along for now. Feigning a yawn, she raised her hands above her head as if stretching as she slowly allowed her eyes to open.

'Feeling better I take it?' he said, motioning his head towards the tray of empty plates and glass that he held out in front of him, like a shield. She dug her hands into the mattress behind her and pushed into an upright position, pasting on a cheerful smile

'Much, thanks to you' she said and watched as his eyes travelled slowly over her, the hair on the back of her neck standing up in awareness. Everywhere his eyes touched, felt like a physical caress across her now overly sensitive skin. Her heart rate and respiration increased, her pulse beat out a rapid tattoo as her blood heated and thickened as it rushed through her veins. He slowly lowered the tray onto her bedside cabinet and leaned towards her, the back of his hand rising towards her forehead.

'May I?' he asked, but it seemed to Kitty that he was asking permission to do far more than check her temperature. She nodded her ascent, her lashes lowering at the feel of his skin against her own, as the back of his hand ran smoothly over her forehead, and she bit her lip on a silent whimper.

Blake had only meant to double check that her fever had gone, or so he told himself. What he was really doing though, was checking his own response to her. He shouldn't touch her, especially not in her bedroom when she was wearing so little, and his control was so thin. She was also recovering from some illness, probably just a chill, but never the less at the moment she was vulnerable. He wasn't being fair and he knew it, but couldn't seem to pull back, his hand brushed her skin and tingles shot up his whole arm. Heard the slight gasp she made as she bit her bottom lip.

He groaned as he watched her small white teeth, bother the succulent flesh. He gave in and lowered his head towards hers, her long lashes fanned onto her know flushed cheeks and he knew without a doubt that this time it wasn't due to a fever, because if it was he'd caught it too.

He could feel his own body reacting to her proximity, her scent enveloped him as he was drawing closer to her luscious mouth. Her pulse beat frantically in her throat as her breathing sped up.

His target changed, he couldn't resist nipping the side of her neck, sucking the skin between his lips and rubbing his tongue over that frantic pulse, in slow circles. He heard her breath hitch and her head moved to one side, allowing him better access. He moved slowly up her neck as he lowered himself onto the mattress on his knees, using an arm as leverage on her other side, hemming her in.

She slipped her arms around his neck as his mouth nibbled a path up throat and over her chin then sipped at the corner of her mouth. He started teasing her mouth with his, biting her lower lip and running his tongue over it. When her mouth opened to him, he slid his tongue inside to taste her, rubbing it along her own questing one. Her hands moved from his neck to his head where they anchored in his hair as the kiss deepened, no body contact apart from mouths. He'd learned his lesson from last time, if they touched anywhere else he'd be lost and this would end as it had in his office with them both spent and still fully clothed, he thought dryly.

Kitty was melting, her body heating as his mouth explored hers with eroticism. She wouldn't need to say anything or try and figure out how to seduce him, he was doing all the work she thought with satisfaction as she let go and sank into his kiss.

Her hands tugged at his hair and he released her mouth and pulled back resting his forehead against hers his breathing ragged and loud to his own ears, as he desperately tried to pull more oxygen into his burning lungs. He needed to slow this down or better yet stop, she'd just spent the last several hours fighting a high temperature and his pride couldn't handle the possibility that she was turning to him in her weakness. He wanted her completely well and giving as well as taking her pleasure and now wasn't that time.

'We need to stop' he groaned his eyes closed tightly as his forehead rested against hers and heard her resigned sigh. His eyes opened and he found himself trapped by her mesmerizing green gaze, the pupils were huge, the gold flecks practically crackling and he cursed himself for a fool for what he knew he was about to do. He knew it was going to leave him aching again but there was no other recourse as far as he was concerned. He was going to have to be strong and protect them both from something she may well regret later.

Kitty could have kicked him, once again he'd gotten her all hot and bothered and the time she'd decided to let go he was going to put the brakes on, well she'd see about that, by god. This time she was going to make sure he finished what he'd started. One hand left his hair and staring into his dark brown eyes she trailed it down over his chest and felt a tremor run through him. His eyelids had drooped, colour slashing his cheekbones and his eyes turned nearly black in his arousal and she grinned.

'Are you sure you want to stop?' she asked as her hand lowed further still and she rubbed him rhythmically through his suit pants, he was thick, long and hard as steel against her. He groaned and his eyes opened widely at the move, his hand moving to trap hers. He was going to hell, he thought as her hand ran lightly over his erection, she was daring him and he never backed down from that, he was going to end what he'd started several nights ago and damn them both. He pulled her hand away from his erection and raised it up towards his mouth where he leisurely sucked each digit into his mouth, swirling his tongue around the tip before allowing it to pop out and move on to the next. When he'd suckled all 5 his mouth trailed over her palm and he bit and then ran his tongue in a circle over the tender pad of flesh beneath her thumb. He watched smugly as the black pupil ate up nearly all her colour and had to clench his jaw to stop the heated growl from leaving his throat.

'I'm trying to be a gentleman here' he added teeth clenched but couldn't resist going a little further, promising himself that he'd stop soon. He pulled the lightweight cover off her and slowly trailed his fingers up her thigh, pushing the material of her large night shirt up to reveal her smooth lithe, golden body.

His thumb skimmed over her flat stomach circling her belly button and on over her ribs as he edged the shirt higher. He finally had it where he wanted it, resting above her lacy pink bra, the tops of her breasts swelled above the scalloped cups and her straining nipples visible as they pushed against the soft material, taunting him. He sat back on his heels so he could view what he'd revealed, then unable to resist the temptation of the bounty before him he pinched the front catch and gave a quick flick of his wrist and watched it part in satisfaction. He now had full access to her full rounded breasts.

He watched her face closely to gauge her reaction as his hand slowly caressed first one breast and then the other. Her nipples went from dusky brown to berry red as he teased them one at a time by rolling and pinching them between his thumb and forefinger. Her pupils expanded fully eating up the entire colour as her arousal increased. His mind was now fully focused on her pleasure. He leaned forward and blew on first one nipple and then the other before slowly running his tongue over them. He sucked first one into his mouth and bit down gently before moving on to give the next one the same attention. He watched her from under his lashes, her eyelids dropped closed and she arched forward pushing them further into his caress.

'We really need to stop now' he said on a groan as once again she found him through his trousers and gave a squeeze, he bit back a curse as he jerked at the sensation, he was going to make her pay for that.

He leaned further into her and suckled more strongly at her left breast and began to knead the right one as his the other hand began a leisurely foray south. His fingertip trailed over her ribs, down her stomach, dipped into her belly button then lowered into the waistband of her small panties and caressed her lightly. He teased circles against her bead and grinned with satisfaction as her hips slowly raised to meet his questing hand. When he had her panting and arching into his movements he stopped and removed his hand from inside her panties and released her nipple with a last lick and sat back up.

'I think I need to leave, before we do something we'll both regret' he told her making as if to get up from the bed.

'Leave me like this and you die' she said between clenched teeth as she launched herself at him, her mouth taking his with more heat than technique. He felt double assaults on his trousers and shirt buttons and grinned wickedly, as he was pushed bodily over as she straddled him, deepening the kiss as her hand loosened the last button on his shirt and he heard his zipper going down.

It seemed playtime was over, he'd managed to press all her aggressive buttons and now he was going to reap his reward and he couldn't wait, his arousal was straining the material of his briefs.

Her hand trailed over the chest she'd revealed complete with more of that ink she'd seen glimpses of at the edge of his rolled up sleeve at dinner. It carried on up on one side of his stomach over one peck, and across his shoulder and down to just past his elbow, dark whorls and intricate tribal markings. Dark hair smattered his chest which was in rather fine shape as was his washboard stomach. She flicked his flat brown nipples with her finger tips and sucked his bottom lip into her mouth as she lowered his zip. She then lowered her pelvis against him and rotated her hips and felt him buck against her and had to bite back a moan as his rock solid erection rubbed against the sensitive bundle of nerves in her sex. She needed to put some space between their lower bodies or she was going to come. She'd be damned if he was still clothed this time so she wrestled him out of his clothes, not that he tried to stop her, far from it.

He was shucking his shoulders out of his shirt at the same time as he kicked off his shoes, toed off his socks and wriggled until his trousers hit the floor. Then his hands were on her t-shirt and he had it pulled over her head taking the time to lean up and take a nipple into his mouth and suckle while her hands were trapped above her head. She threw it off her head and her bra dropped behind her as her arms fell again and her hair landed around them in a black fan. She arched down into his caress the movement making her hair tickle his thighs erotically.

He used her disadvantage against her and rolled her on to her back as he came down beside her, pushing his hand into the waistband of her panties and then pushing them down so he could get unhindered access to her. He tested her readiness and found her slick and wet on his fingers. He brought the wet digits to his mouth and licked the evidence off as he watched her eyelids lower and her mouth part as she panted. He used his feet to push her panties further down her legs and she flicked them off over her feet to fall on the floor. She in turned pushed down his briefs and as his erection sprang free she took him into her hot little hand and stroked him, just a gliding of her palm up and down a few times and his control snapped.

He pushed her hand away and placed them over her head, then pressed down on her hands, a silent request to keep them there while he positioned himself. He held onto her hips as he entered her in one thrust. They groaned in unison at the sensation of him sliding smoothly inside her to the hilt. She was so wet, the feeling so overwhelming for him that he forgot all about finesse and technique and just began to pump into her like a piston. His body so ready for release it was painful and he could feel the tingling begin in the base of his back.

Her legs curled around his waist as she arched up to meet his every downward thrust, her hands lifted from over her head and pulled his face down to hers. She thrust her tongue into his mouth mimicking the actions of their lower bodies and he felt her inner muscles tighten around him. She stiffened against him as she arched up and groaned into his mouth as her climax hit. She was so tight, the exquisite sensation of her internal muscles clamping down threw him violently over the edge with her to a shuddering release, his body emptying inside her. He collapsed on her his breathing ragged as his abused lungs finally got the much needed oxygen they'd been denied. He hadn't been able to catch his breath his release had been so intense it had shocked him, stealing his breath. He felt her relax beneath him as her legs loosened their death grip and dropped to either side of his hips. Her hands falling limply over her head as she too struggled to catch her breath. He wanted to see her face, needed to make sure he hadn't hurt her, but would admit to a little trepidation over what he'd see in her eyes.

Would there be anxiety overlaying her satisfaction, like the episode in his office, meaning he'd find himself bare arsed on the floor, or would she lie replete in his arms this time?

He really wanted to just lie down for a while and hold her, something he usually avoided at all costs. His brain fog finally began to clear as the blood slowly returned, with it the realisation that they'd just had unprotected sex. That was something he'd never done before, not even his first time, as a Gorky teenager. His head dropped onto her chest and he groaned as he called himself all the stupid names he could think of. How could he have been so irresponsible, he'd been so lost in the moment that he'd forgotten? There again it had been overwhelming, she was the only woman who'd ever made him lose control.

Also the only one who left his body utterly spent and completely satisfied too when he was with her, or thought about her green eyes. He sheepishly recalled, memories surfacing of how he'd been getting off over the last 18 months or so with his lovers, but he pushed it away for now, not wanting to analyse it.

Kitty heard Blake groan against her and frowned, the sound infiltrating her haze, it had been absolutely amazing and he was ruining the mood.

'What?' she asked as she slowly raised her heavy hand and ran it through his damp hair lifting it off his forehead so she could see his face

'I didn't use protection' he said turning his head to the side, sounding disgusted. She smiled and kissed his rough cheek at his petulant tone, he was worried over nothing and relaxed again. He pulled himself up on his arms as he felt her hand run soothingly through his hair and the soft touch of her lips against his cheek. She was reacting so much better than she had at his office and he was tempted to just let all his worries go, did he really want to rock the boat here? After all, all he really wanted to do was stay exactly where he was, still enveloped in her body completely. Then he groaned again as his conscience pricked him, he wanted, no needed to see her face.

As he pulled up onto his arms he watched her eyes open slowly to meet his, they were heavy lidded and she looked sleepy and completely satisfied. Best of all she wasn't hissing at him or trying to shove him off, then he remembered the lack of protection.

'Did you hear what I said?' he asked and frowned as she just nodded and turned onto her side, dislodging him and pushing him onto his back roughly, before curling up against his side, resting her head on his chest and a hand on his stomach. This was just how he'd imagined lying with her earlier, the only thing marring it was her complete lack of worry over his announcement.

'You're not concerned?' he asked, he didn't know why he couldn't let it go, well apart from the obvious, she seemed fine about it; so why should he let it bother him? But he did. He felt the hand that had been resting on his stomach start to draw small circles around his tattoo as she shook her head. He put a hand under her chin, something wasn't right here, he could sense it and he put a hand under her stubborn chin and lifted her face up so he could look into it and was shocked to see the depth of sorrow shining in her eyes.

'I can't get pregnant' she informed him then her eyes skittered away and he had to admit to being stunned, he'd expected to hear her say she was on some form of contraception, after all she'd been with Edmonton up to a few days ago, but not that, never that.

Kitty watched him scowl and didn't like it. 'What are you thinking about?' she asked suspiciously and he looked down into her face again

'Did you use protection with Edmonton?' he knew he sounded like a jealous arse, he really did but the thought of her sharing pleasure, skin to skin contact with him made his gut's twist and his jealousy flare. She snorted, then laughed and he raised a sardonic brow in silent query, not really trusting himself to speak

'I never slept with Lance' she said indignantly, "what sort of woman did he take her for? Thinking that she went from one mans bed to another" and snapped 'I'm not a hussy or a moron' he looked at her in surprise and she sighed raising herself up so they were eye to eye.

'He sleeps around, I don't' she said as if that should be answer enough. He frowned at her logic; she thought he slept around or so she'd said the other day, and watched as she rolled her eyes at his bewilderment. She needed to clear something up.

'I'd only had a couple of dates with Lance, I needed more time to get to know him' she explained, then her brow wrinkled in confusion as she thought that she'd just had sex with Blake after only a couple of days, and a business date, not even a real one. Well she'd worked for him for 2 years, but that didn't really qualify did it? This was a whole new level. She heard him sigh and looked up at him again as she wondered where her common sense was where he was concerned? What was it about him that made her lose all perspective?

'I haven't slept with all the women I've dated' he informed her and watched the incredulity cross her face. He growled 'I'm not Edmonton' and pulled her back down onto his chest, he liked her there and he didn't want to argue.

'Let's forget all about him' he added feeling the pressure in his chest ease and he smiled to himself knowing that Edmonton had never seen her like this, had never felt this connection with her. He couldn't help it, he felt smug and self-satisfied at the thought, then registered what she'd said and frowned?

'So would you like to explain to me exactly what you meant?' he said quietly and felt her stiffen against him and rubbed her shoulder to try and offer comfort and support.

She slowly began to relax against him as the soothing motion of his hand began to ease the tension from her body. She couldn't believe that she'd blurted it out the way she had, it wasn't something she usually brought up voluntarily. She also knew that now she had she owed him an explanation. She couldn't blame him for his curiosity, maybe he thought she was feeding him a line, trying to trap him and frowned at the thought, would he think that? Then shrugged away the unpleasant thought, she knew the truth, could even back it up with medical evidence but now wasn't the time. He was waiting patiently for an answer, she sighed in resignation, if she'd just kept her big mouth shut then she wouldn't be in this position. Typical example of brain and filter where he was concerned. She could have told him she was on birth control, that would have been the easiest route to go, but when had the truth ever been easy?

She rubbed her cheek distractedly against his chest hair, enjoying the feeling of the soft, springy hair tickling her cheek. She inhaled his now familiar scent as she took strength from his closeness.

'The simple truth is I was born with only one ovary and it doesn't work very well' she said 'If I got pregnant naturally it would be a miracle', it had never really bothered her before but for some reason at this time and with this man, it really did.

Blake gave her a comforting hug and rubbed his chin against her hair deep in thought. He hadn't been expecting that answer, was shocked to hear it especially coupled with the resignation in her voice, his heart ached for her. How hard must it be to know that you'd never be able to make a new life with the person you loved? It must have been a bitter pill to swallow. It wasn't something he usually thought about, well apart from the unsettling vision he'd had of Kitty being ripe with his child earlier when he'd thought about his sister's pregnancy. It must be damn near impossible for her to let herself get close to someone already knowing that there was going to be fertility issues. Most people didn't have that kind of knowledge at the start of a relationship. It was usually something that was discovered after a couple started to have problems conceiving. It must be terrifying going into a new relationship knowing that if it things looked like they were turning serious, she was eventually going to have to explain her medical condition. He didn't see it as a deficiency or something that would put anyone off, it was just something that would have to be discussed, solutions sought or compromises made.

'So are the doctors 100% sure?' he asked, he didn't know why he was so interested, it wasn't as if he was looking to start a family, he was just curious. She went so quiet he couldn't even

hear her breathing and he could have kicked himself, how unfeeling could he have sounded?
He knew it must be painful to talk about, so why the hell was he pushing? He was just about to apologise for his tactless questioning when her he heard her take a breath and her hand started stroking circles on his stomach again.

'Well no, nothing is 100%' she said then added in a very sleepy voice 'it's just that it's highly improbable that with the problems I have, that the one and only time I have unprotected sex I'd end up pregnant' she explained as she fought to keep her eyes open. Her lids had become heavy and she yawned loudly, she wanted this conversation over, was finding it rather distressing. She didn't know why? It was something she thought she'd come to terms with years ago and it wasn't as if it was pertinent to what was happening between them. It was much too early in the game to consider possible long term commitments and problems. Fatigue started to take its toll and her eyes started to drift closed against her will as the heat from his warm skin begin to penetrate her chilled body. Funny she hadn't even felt herself cooling it must have been the topic?

'I don't normally have unprotected sex' she said her voice starting to slur 'I don't normally get carried away either?' she added and he could feel her frown against him just before her breath evened out and she fell asleep.

He ached for her he really did, it was a hard enough decision to make in the first place, to commit your life to someone else. But to know that you were going to tie your life, your future to someone you couldn't give children to, must be extremely difficult. He gave up his musings as he himself yawned, he tugged the blanket over them both and drifted off to sleep, content with Kitty curled up against him.

Chapter Twelve

When Kitty woke a couple of hours later, the bed felt empty and cold and Blake was missing. She got up, slipped on a warm dressing gown and slippers and eventually tracked him down in the kitchen. He was dressed and sitting at the kitchen table nursing a cup of coffee. As she entered he got up and kissed her lightly on the forehead, made her sit down and then set a cup of coffee and another omelette down in front of her. He waited with her while she ate and then cleared up after her. He assured himself that she was fine and on the mend, then made his excuses and left.

Blake hadn't really wanted to leave her alone but the fact that he enjoyed being around her as much as he did and not just in bed was enough to spook him. As soon as he'd assured himself that she was on the mend, her fever gone, he'd made some excuse about pressing matters he needed to attend to and left. He just needed to put a little space between them to get some perspective on what was happening to him. He'd freaked himself out when he'd woken up wrapped around her, he'd never fallen asleep with his partners after sex. Once the glow wore off and before the sheets cooled he was usually gone, waking up with her in his arms had felt too right to him and he'd panicked. He'd managed to slip out of bed quietly without disturbing her and had donned his creased clothes and escaped into the kitchen by himself to make a coffee.

It was 8 in the evening, he'd slept far longer and a lot deeper than he normally did and he didn't know what the hell was happening to him? He didn't normally get affected by women but Kitty wasn't a normal woman and he didn't react to her like he did to others. All he'd wanted to do was wake her up and start all over again, even down to sleeping with her and it had scared the hell out of him.

Kitty hadn't seen Blake since he'd left her flat late in the evening the night before last. He'd assured himself that she was more or less back to normal before leaving. He'd had a few things to do and a couple of calls to make and it had been getting late when he'd finally left. She was surprised he'd waited for her to wake up to be honest; she'd expected him to have done a runner as soon as her eyes had closed. Maybe he really was who she hoped he was and had spent Friday just pottering around at home, reading and watching television.

She'd felt wonderful when she'd woken this morning, her energy levels renewed and her body wonderfully relaxed, it seemed good sex was beneficial. It must have just been a chill she'd pick up because her temperature hadn't returned.

She'd decided that trying to hide her identity was a moot point now, the truth would come out eventually it usually did. So she'd visited a little boutique in Altringham in the afternoon looking for something nice to wear to the Art gallery. She'd promised to lend her support to Audrey and Dan. She'd purchased a little green cocktail dress that had a fitted bodice with shoestring straps and a handkerchief hem that ended just above her knees in a swirl of material. She'd also found a pair of silver sandals that matched the thread woven through the material of the little dress and a spangled silver comb to secure her hair off her face but had not worn it, instead leaving it down.

She now stood near one of the pillars that were dotted around, feeling rather conspicuous without her usual armour, while she sipped at a mineral water, not wanting to upset her stomach after Thursday.

Dan and Audrey were working the room, just a few feet away trying to boost sales, not that his work needed a hard sale, he was a very talented artist. His vision and clarity suffused his paintings and his natural warmth of character was also felt within each of the pieces, they left you with a feeling of lightness and clarity. Her eye had been taken by one in particular, done in tones of lavender, gold and cream that would look spectacular on the wall opposite her bed. The piece spoke to her on a subconscious level and the simple, light brush strokes and smooth curves and angles had left her with a feeling of deep peace and tranquillity. Exactly right for a bedroom, to aid in restful sleep, she'd thought. She was happy to see her red sold spot on the bottom right hand corner as the picture had had quite a few interested parties.

She leaned against the pillar as she took another sip of her sparkling drink as Blake appeared on the other side and settled himself in an identical pose to her. He had observed her for a while before he'd finally given in and made his way over, he hadn't seen her since he'd left her on Thursday evening. He'd been out of the office on Friday and had left a message for her to take the day off to fully recover.

She looked spectacular in the little green dress that was moulded to her breasts and showed off her spectacular hour glass figure, her silver sandals offering a glimpse of her dainty feet and her pretty painted, pink toenails. Her hair hung down her back in a shiny black wave moving as if alive with her elegant movements as she'd moved around the floor earlier, chatting to various people and discussing Dan's work. He hadn't lasted long, it had only taken 2 or 3 men's eyes following her progress to raise his hackles and as soon as she'd settled against the pillar, he'd made his way over to her not wanting to give them an opening to make a move on her.

He raised his champagne flute to her in a silent toast to their relationship, trying not to make it obvious to all and sundry by keeping a discreet distance between them, but knowing instinctively it would be close enough to give a warning to other interested males. He didn't think he would be able to keep his hands to himself if he got too close to her his resistance was at an all-time low.

He'd been annoyed to find that his bed had felt too big without her there, not that she'd ever been there or any other woman for that matter.

It was that he'd slept better with her tucked against him than he'd done once he was home, for the first time in his 32 years he wanted to bring a woman into his private space. She smiled shyly at him and he grinned back at her. He let loose a good natured chuckle as he spotted Audrey looking their way, her eyes were moving from one to the other in suspicion, then she beamed a quick flash of her teeth. She bent down to kiss her husband Dan on the top of his greying strawberry blonde hair as he sat in his chair in animated conversation with a couple. His hand patted her retreating rear as she walked away, he'd hit dead on target without stopping the flow of conversation or turning his eyes.

Blake grinned again, the man seemed to have the innate ability to know exactly where his wife was at any given moment. He liked him he wasn't flamboyant or arrogant as some artist could be. He was outgoing and friendly and a damn fine artist, he already had several of his water colours strategically placed around his home, Dan's work the only personal touches he'd added in his austere apartment.

Audrey stopped just before the pillar, looking from one to the other with a speculative gleam in her eye and then she let loose a laugh. Kitty could feel her cheeks heating under her scrutiny.

'You do know that you're making it blatantly obvious that you have an intimate relationship purely by the fact that you are trying so desperately to appear like you've not' she told them. Blake was taken aback, he wasn't use to feeling foolish, he hadn't credited that Audrey would pick up on his subtle warning to other males. Women were usually unaware of the intricacies that went on with men but as usual he'd underestimated her, the woman was a blood hound and seemed to have a sixth sense when it came to people. He was not one for public displays of affection, he didn't usually feel comfortable with them but he had a feeling his life was about to change in ways he'd never thought possible.

'Took you long enough to notice her' she whispered in Blake's ear' as she stood on tip toe then kissed his cheek and patted his shoulder as if in sympathy. She grabbed Kitty's free hand and tugged her from the other side of the pillar and then nodded with satisfaction as Blake gave in to his need and settled his hand around her waist. 'Much better' she said then beamed at them both as if they'd done something very clever.

'He's already sold half of his paintings' she said as she sipped her own champagne and grabbed a handful of tiny sandwiches off a passing waiter, watching her husband with pride as he spoke to a middle aged couple. 'The sculptures are nearly all sold too' she added with pride. Blake and Kitty had to agree that the man was extremely talented the sculptures were very delicate, each one a small figurine, made with exquisite attention to detail and each one unique and represented hope over adversity. One was of a couple embracing as they danced the man had a prosthetic arm wrapped around her. Another was of a man in a wheelchair and his partner sat on his lap her head back and looking as if she'd been caught in a moment of merriment as the man looked on lovingly. But Blake's absolute favourite and the one that now carried his red dot was that of a little boy, strapped into a set of leg braces and chasing a football with a large happy smile on his angelic face. It was an absolutely stunning piece and he'd had to have it once he'd seen it. It had reminded him of a similarly inspirational scene he'd come across when jogging one day in the park.

A little boy of about 5 or 6 years old had been holding onto a walking frame, his lower legs strengthened in braces as he chased his older brother, he could still hear their laughter if he closed his eyes. The child had looked so happy and carefree that the disability had been outshone by his pure joy of life. He'd found the scene inspiring, it was at the very beginning when he'd just started out. He'd been strapped for cash, physically exhausted and worrying that he'd ever make it.

The little boy had reminded him that anything is possible if you want it badly enough, it had bolstered him to go that extra mile and the following year with Greg's help he'd had his first breakthrough. After that as they say, he'd never looked back. Seeing the piece had reminded him of those early days, when only his ability to laugh at his circumstances and his need to provide a better future for him, his mum and sister had kept him going. He needed to make sure he didn't forget that now, and he was hoping that the piece would act as his inspiration. He was determined that he would now spend more time looking for the simple inexpensive pleasures that life and family had to offer and not get so lost in the rest.

The 3 of them were discussing the charity when Blake spotted several women looking to a point over his shoulder, his curiosity got the better of him and he turned to look. Near the door stood an older version of the young man in Kitty's photo. He nudged her to get her attention and she looked at him enquiringly.

'Look towards the door' he said and watched as she turned, her face split into a breath taking smile and he felt jealousy rear its ugly head, it wasn't something he was use to feeling but he wanted her to light up like that when she looked at him.

Kitty waved to get Rob's attention and he raised his hand in acknowledgement and made his way through the crowd, smiling and moving around people to get to her.

'Hey kitten' he said picking her up and squeezing her. Audrey's brows hit her hairline as she watched the man pull Kitty into his arms, he was the most attractive man she'd ever seen, jet black hair and sculptured features were utter perfection. Then his long black eyelashes lifted and she actually sucked in a breath as she spotted his absolutely stunning golden eyes.

'Audrey, meet my big brother Rob' Kitty said as way of introduction and Audrey's mouth opened in surprise as she looked towards Blake, and watched the smug smile tug his lips as he licked his finger and lifted it in the air and gave a downward motion. She growled at him as he burst out laughing, he was enjoying Audrey's discomfort in her reaction to the man's looks and the realization that he was not competition for Blake. He watched her blush and had to bite his lip to keep his laughter back as Rob lifted her hand to his mouth and kissed the back of her hand in an old courtly manner.

The woman had a trim figure and her auburn bob was artfully coloured, her make-up was tasteful but she was in her mid-50's, but was blushing like a virgin because a good looking man had kissed the back of her hand. He couldn't blame her though, even he could admit that the man had astonishing looks, perfectly sculptured facial features and his eyes were something else to behold up close. He'd be worried if he wasn't her brother, he was honest enough to admit.

'I hardly think 6 hours constitutes older' Rob said dryly as he turned to look suspiciously at Blake. He managed to stop the stunned expression from showing that not only was he her brother, but that he was also her twin. She hadn't told him but there again they hadn't really spoken much at all and Kitty never about anything really personal, apart from her fertility issues. He'd given her a rundown of his family history but she hadn't reciprocated.

They would have to rectify that he thought with frustration, he really didn't like being caught on the hop. Blake took the proffered hand and introduced himself as Rob pointedly gave him the once over taking in the fact that he'd placed his hand back around Kitty's waist.

He released Blake's hand and turned stonily to his sister and spoke lowly to her in what sounded like rapid Italian. Blake and Audrey's eyebrows rose as Kitty scowled at him and then reciprocated heatedly in the same language. 'Oh they really did need to talk she definitely hadn't put that on her resume'. He'd caught the gist of the disagreement though. Rob now knew that Blake was her boss and was not happy about it, especially as he was seeing her outside of work. Kitty was trying to tell him to mind his own business, that wasn't going to work, it wouldn't have worked with him either, if it came to Mel and they weren't twins.

'Basta cosi!' she snapped and stamped on Robs foot in frustration and he scowled at her as he stepped back out of range. 'English only, don't be so rude' she said and gave him a sweet smile. Blake tugged on her waist to bring her in closer to his side as he could feel her about to explode and he lowered his mouth to her ear.

'Put the claws away Kitty, he's just looking out for you' he said then placed a gentle kiss on the side of her neck before raising his head and looking her angry brother in the eye.

'Yes, she's my personal assistant but me dating her and her position are not relative. I have never dated an employee before, ever' he emphasized the last word.

He was not impressed at having to explain himself, especially in public but he had to concede that in this case it was probably the most expedient way of cooling the situation down. Kitty looked ready to stamp on her brother again and by the vicious look in her eye it wouldn't be his foot she'd go for next time. He must admit to finding the situation amusing, how the hell he hadn't guessed that there was Italian in her blood, was beyond him. The passion and colouring alone should have thrown up warning signs. He'd been oblivious though as neither Kitty nor her brother had accents until they spoke it?

'Okay, fine, I'll stop the big brother act' Rob conceded Then grinned at her and pulled her hair before bursting into raucous laughter as she punched him in the arm, as if they were children.

'God I really don't see what women see in you?' she hissed in disgust as she took a sip of her soda, wishing desperately that it was something stronger at the moment. Audrey snorted

'Please the man is gorgeous, what's not to like?' she grinned her sense of humour returned. Rob bowed low over her hand 'see a woman of great taste' he winked at Blake over her head.

'You really have a death wish?' Blake said laughing at his antics, the mood lightening around them. Kitty began to relax against him and smiled at her brother.

'Let Audrey show you around and introduce you to her fabulously talented husband Dan, the artist'. He politely held out his elbow for her and Audrey happily put her hand through it as she led him to her husband. They watched Dan finish up his present conversation with an enthusiastic collector as his wife and Rob approached him.

Blake watched Dan smile and take the hand offered by Rob as Audrey introduced them. Then he watched Dan frown as he looked over the man in front of him. Rob must have said something because the frown cleared and Dan started to speak animatedly himself, his arms gesticulating wildly as he laughed. He watched Audrey relax against her husband's side, resting her bottom on the arm of his wheelchair as his arm wrapped around her waist. They seemed completely as ease with each other and he looked down at Kitty who was watching them with a warm smile.

He bent his head down to her ear

'Come home with me tonight?' he whispered and kissed her neck quickly before straitening again, he wasn't usually comfortable with public displays but he'd been stood with his arm around her waist for some time now, he had no idea what had gotten into him?.

'Come on let's circulate' he said 'while you think about how good I can make you feel later' he grinned down at her beaming face as they started to move through the room. They spotted Alison Pope; Len Simpson's secretary in training, stood in a corner on her own, quietly examining a stunning picture in bright autumn colours, she was so engrossed in the painting that she jumped when Kitty touched her arm.

'Oh hi' she smiled shyly at them and Kitty watched her beautiful violet eyes widen in horror at something over her shoulder.

'I read the minutes of Thursday's meeting you did for me' Blake said oblivious to her discomfort 'you did brilliantly, I think Len's going to be lucky to have you once Mavis retires' he told her and Kitty watched as warm colour travelled into her cheeks. She was painfully shy and Kitty felt sorry for her, she seemed mostly lost to her.

'Hi, I'm Rob, Kitty's brother' she heard as her brother's hand appeared around her, she noticed his voice had lowered and her hackles rose, as he waited patiently for Alison to reciprocate. She watched her roll her lips inwards in uncertainty, then her lashes lifted revealing the stunning colour of her eyes as her hand came out tentatively and took his waiting one.

'I'm Alison, I work for one of Blake's directors' she explained and smiled shyly, a dimple appearing in her cheek and her eyes turning lavender in her flushed face and Kitty heard Rob's breath catch. She looked over to Alison as she released his hand

'Excuse me a moment will you? I just need a quick word with my brother' she said gently and then to Blake 'would you mind? I won't be a moment' she added and pointedly looked towards Alison. He caught on to the fact that there was something amiss with the way her brother had reacted and gently took Alison by the elbow to lead her over to take a look at the sculptures.

'Oh no you don't' she hissed at Rob as she looked around making sure they weren't overheard 'She's not one of your playthings' she added 'she's shy and sweet and extremely lovely, she also hasn't dated since she lost her husband 3 years ago' she told him as he looked at her solemnly. His eyes followed the pretty, petite brunette as Blake spoke to her about the sculptures, her face rapt with interest as he explained something to her.

'I was just being friendly' he told her defensively and Kitty snorted 'This is me you're talking to! I know the old octave lowering trick' she told him and watched his brows rise and laughed 'please, give me some credit, we spent way too much time together for me to miss any of your tricks' she said 'I love you

Rob, I really do but you would scare her to death, she isn't equipped to deal with someone with your skills and reputation' she added and he growled.

'I'm not a complete bastard you know, she just looked lost, there's just something about her?' he said and shrugged his shoulders shoving his hands in his trouser pockets. Kitty looked at him with interest

'And what about the little plaything you've left warming your bed?' she asked and he had the grace to colour

'I never took her there in the first place' he admitted sheepishly and heard her shocked intake of breath 'she was all looks and no substance' he said and grinned at her incredulous face 'I do have some morale's Kitten, I'd at least like to be able to have a very basic conversation with someone I'm about to get intimate with' and it was her turn to colour 'I do like to talk to them occasionally' he said dryly then took her arm and urged her after Blake.

'Come on let's go spend some time with your lover' and he watched colour infuse her face in guilt 'Argh, so you've already done the nasty have you?' he teased and watched the colour reach her hair line 'that good huh' he laughed as he tugged her along ignoring her muttering 'Oh come on sis, lighten up it's about time you found someone who knows what to do in bed' and she sputtered as he ignored her and carried on 'oh please, do you think I was deaf, the only groaning I ever heard coming from your room was Nathan' he nudged her and whistled innocently under his breath as she stopped in her tracks.

She was mortified that her brother was aware of her sex life, silly she knew but there you go. He grabbed her hand and dragged her along with him. 'Oh chill out' he said as he walked towards the display case that Blake and Alison were stood looking at.

Blake looked up as she reached his side and he pulled her into him 'everything okay?' he asked, she was looking a little flushed, his hand automatically reached up to check her temperature, thinking it had come back and Rob set off laughing behind her.

'She's not ill, I'm afraid I embarrassed her' he added unrepentant and moved to Alison's side, making sure he put his hands in his pockets. Blake looked towards Kitty and back to Rob with a raised brow.

'I'll tell you later' she said and he squeezed her waist

'Good, at least I know I'm getting a later' he added with a lascivious grin and she heard Rob cough and shake his head. He grinned over at his sister's scarlet face again and waggled his brows suggestively before he turned his attention back to something Alison was saying.

'God he's annoying' she said but there was no heat in her words 'and yes you get a later' she added as she stood on tiptoe and gave in to the need to kiss him lightly. He didn't pull away as she thought he'd do but captured her lips with his own in a quick heated kiss before turning his attention back to the sculptures.

They all stayed together for another hour talking pleasantly and enthusing over the success of the sales before Blake made his excuses to Audrey as he placed Kitty's wrap around her shoulders and ushered her out. Rob had stayed behind to take a call and Alison had walked on ahead, she stood near the kerb looking hopefully towards the taxis. Kitty was just about to ask Blake if they could take her home on their way when Rob appear behind them and spoke up

'I'll drop Alison off on the way back to my hotel, it's on my way' he said and took her arm to usher her to his Audi, surprisingly she didn't protest, just smiled gratefully and waved happily at Kitty and Blake as Rob helped her into his car and drove away.

Kitty was quiet in the car and Blake let her be for now, they could talk once they got to his apartment. He was looking forward to sleeping wrapped around her and this time he didn't freak out about it.

He pulled into the underground parking at his apartment block

'Isn't this one of the places you own?' she added as he helped her out of the car.

'Yes, one of the first, it was originally the site of an old abandoned warehouse, the land and building a complete eyesore as it attracted vandals'

'Wow it certainly isn't now' she said 'I'd love to get a look at the grounds?' He made a sound of none committal, as he ushered her into the lift and pressed the button for the top floor. He pulled her into his arms and gave into the need to kiss her properly. It had driven him to distraction having to keep up with the required friendly conversation all evening. He'd been conscious of her every movement at his side as they'd circulated and chatted and he'd been in a constant state of arousal even before that.

He'd been speechless when he'd first spotted her standing in the middle of the room, her hair flowing down her back and the little cocktail dress drawing his attention to the figure hugging bodice before it had skimmed her hips and stopped just above her knee.

For him she was the highlight of his night, the most beautiful item in the room.

He groaned into her mouth as it opened to his touch. He wanted to go slowly, perhaps play some soothing music as he showed her the view from his balcony. That would have to wait, he felt starved, as if it had been months instead of just over 24 hours since he'd felt her naked against him. The lift doors opened and they nearly fell out as he had her pinned against the door. She giggled as he grabbed her hand and pulled her at a fast clip towards his front door.

It was only feet away from the lift but it was taking too long so Blake scooped her up in his arms as he swiped his card against the lock and the door opened. He kicked it closed and carried her through the apartment in the dark, straight into his bedroom. He tormented them both by slowly sliding her body down his own as he lowered her to her feet in front of him and stepped back.

She reached up to loosen his tie and then caught hold of both ends and used it to drag him down to her hungry waiting mouth. His hand busy behind her, lowering the zip on her dress and then pushing the tiny shoestring straps off her shoulders and breaking the kiss so his mouth could follow the progress of the left strap as it slowly lowered down her arm before dropping off her completely and landing at her feet in a puddle. He wrapped his hands around her waist and lifted her out of the material and lay her down in the middle of his bed. All she had on was a skimpy pair of sheer emerald panties and her silver sandals, he went to drop to his knees on the floor but she leaned up on her elbows and tutted.

'Strip' she demanded and he did in 10 seconds flat, his dress pants and shirt hitting the carpet and landing on her discarded dress. He had to sit on the bed to remove his socks and shoes, he was shaking so badly with desire his legs threatened to give out he was so turned on by her.

Kitty was mesmerized at his body, she watched in rapt fascination, licking her lips in appreciation as his amazing chest and stomach appeared with all that black ink, as his shirt and pants were discarded. He sat next to her as he removed his socks and shoes and she went to get up off the bed, he waylaid her with a hand on her hip as he got to his feet and shrugged his briefs off. His erection thick and heavy as it stood out proudly from his body, she slowly reached out and ran a fingertip over the rigid flesh as he hissed in a breath and lowered himself to his knees and pushed himself between her splayed legs as she fell backwards on the bed before him.

Her head lifted to look at him, her eyes blazing with arousal as he ran his knuckles over her panties and her breasts rose sharply at the brief contact. Her head rested back against the bed as he slowly ran his hand up her stomach and found her left breast as his right continued to rub his knuckles over her sex in small little circular motions.

He groaned and his erection kicked up as he felt how damp she was, he leaned forward and suckled her straight through the material her moans music to his ears as he removed the hand from her breast to scramble around the floor trying to find the condoms he'd placed in his wallet before leaving. He sighed and continued to nuzzle her as he quickly found one, ripped it from the foil and donned it, all in one smooth move.

He pulled himself up onto his knees and pulled her bottom to the edge of the bed, pushed her panties to one side and thrust into her arching body. He had to hold her still as she began to roll her hips against him and had to take several deep breaths to hold off his release. His control hanging by a thread as he pulled her up, so he could suckle her breasts as he moved languidly inside her body. Wrong move he found as she sat up and wrapped her legs around his back, her heels digging into his bottom and the new position pushed him even deeper inside her. They both groaned and the leisurely love making he'd planned went nuclear as they strained together both fighting for release, a couple of frenzied thrusts and it was all over.

They lay slumped together their breathing loud and he felt her shake against him, he pulled back thinking he'd hurt her and found her biting her lip to hold back her laughter. She pushed his hair off his forehead and kissed him tenderly.

'I'm sorry it's just that it's always so quick and overwhelming with us' she told him

'This time yes, but now we've taken the edge off, we'll take it slower' he said as he kissed her eyelids and nose 'and you can teach me some pillow Italian' he said as his mouth took hers again on a groan.

'I have something even better to teach you' she told him huskily as they broke apart, There was very little talking as she removed one condom and replaced it with another she found in the box on the bedside cabinet.

This time Kitty was in the driving seat and she blew his mind with her innate sensuality as she took him apart and left him panting and boneless.

Chapter Thirteen

Kitty sat sipping her coffee huddled up in a blanket on Blake's balcony, wearing nothing but one of Blake's shirts and a pair of his socks. The view of the gardens 12 floors below them was breath-taking. He'd used extremely talented landscapers to make the most of the available space. You would never have known that all of this had once been a derelict warehouse and parking lot to look at it now. It had lush borders and seating areas dotted about the well-tended lawns or wrapped around the various dotted trees, the paths were made of red brick and the centre piece was a fountain surrounded by a profusion of tiered flower urns.

Blake walked out onto his balcony and felt his chest ease, he'd had to step into his office and deal with an emergency and he'd feared she'd be gone when he finally finished an hour later. But there she was curled up on a sofa on the covered in balcony, wearing nothing but one of his shirts and snuggled into a warm blanket as she sipped on a steaming drink. He sniffed appreciatively at the aromatic coffee as he walked towards her. He'd showered and dressed in comfortable jeans and a dark jumper as the air was a little fresh today, he poured himself a coffee out of the pot she'd left on the table and sat down beside her. He drank quietly as she put her feet on his lap and he stroked them distractedly as he relaxed back into the seat allowing the company and scene to blow away the stressful mess he'd just dealt with.

'So when are you going to fill me in on your family?' he asked casually not looking at her but feeling her stiffen as he continued to rub her feet. He heard her take a breath and sigh.

'What would you like to know?' she asked 'you've already met my twin brother' and he smiled at the thought of that meeting and what had followed afterwards.

'Anything you're comfortable sharing' he admitted, he was quite happy for her to take her time and tell him when she was ready. He was convinced now that they had lots of it ahead of them, possibly even a lifetime if he could get her to let down her guard properly.

Kitty sat up and placed her cup on the table, her earlier relaxed mood forgotten as she fretted over how much to tell him? Could she really trust him with the whole truth she wondered? And bit her lip in indecision as she stared intently at him. He sat still under her scrutiny waiting for her to decide if she could trust him, he knew instinctively that she didn't do it often or wholly and he was hoping she would do both with him.

He let out a relieved breath as he heard her sigh as she pulled her feet off his knee and turned around to curl against him. He wrapped his arm around her waist and lifted her bodily onto his lap so he could surround her completely and offer whatever comfort he could. He knew she didn't find this easy.

Kitty took in his comforting scent and decided the beginning was the best place, so taking a big breath and an even bigger leap of faith she plunged in.

'My father is Antonio, Roberto filipo the 3rd duco (duke) of San Domino; it's the biggest of the islands, off the Tremiti islands just off the coast of the Adriatic Sea in Italy'

Blake clamped down on any reaction as the niggling he'd had at the back of his mind suddenly cleared. That's why the picture had been familiar, he'd seen a similar one of her parents but when they were much younger in an old article, he'd been doing some research on possible properties in Italy. He'd come across an old microfiche article in the library as he'd looked into various possible locations before the Bellville had become available and he'd decided that it was better to offer regeneration in his own country.

He remembered reading about a young Italian duke that had supposedly dishonoured his family. For his supposed crime he'd been disinherited and stripped of his title, position, wealth and job after marrying an underwear model. That's who she had reminded him of, her mother, he'd seen pictures of her in several old magazines, she had her features, hair and figure, just her father's colouring. He'd even found an entry later on where his father had tried to sue him for breach of contract, one that had been drawn up on his birth by the families concerned. They'd negotiated a marriage between him and a Contessa that was to take place by his 25th birthday. He'd found it all rather outlandish and barbaric at the time but he supposed that these things still went on in certain circles.

'I've come across the story' he admitted and felt her stiffen and tightened his arms around her to stop her bolting 'if it's any consolation I thought it was a despicable thing for a father to do, I was rather shocked that such outdated and barbaric practices are still allowed to be carried out in this day and age' he added and felt her relax against him.

'My grandfather is a nasty, vindictive, greedy old man, he has never forgiven my father for marrying mum and he's refused to acknowledge both mine and Robs birth' she said 'although he did try and hatch a plot to snatch us when we were little. He thought he could use us as a bargaining chip to pressure dad into divorcing. He thought her beneath him, a taint to his blue blood. What he never bothered to find out was that mum's history lies within Persian royalty on her mother's side, but that's another story'

'Ah, so that's where the golden eyes originate from' he added another mystery solved.

'Anyway he wanted to force him into marrying the much older duchess after the divorce' she heard Blake swear viciously and squeezed his arm to show she appreciated his support.

'His father was title rich but land and scruples poor' she added dryly 'she had a very lucrative piece of land complete with tourist properties and he wanted to get his hands on the money it brought in' She sighed at his thoroughly corrupt conscience.

'Of course what he didn't expect was that the duchess would tell dad after she stumbled upon the plot, they'd kept in touch you see, were friends actually. She didn't want the marriage either, she'd become accustomed to her own council and refused to give up her freedom and wealth to adhere to her deceased father's wishes' she said. 'Plus she already had a secret female lover who just happened to work for my grandfather' she added with a grin as his eyes widened with understanding, it seemed her lover didn't want to lose her either and had used her position to spy.

'Dad was left penniless of course and mum had to continue modelling in the early years of their marriage to keep them going, well until she got pregnant with us' she added 'Poor dad worked long hours for little pay waiting tables and any other job he could find where he could work under the table in Sicily' she silently fumed at the unfairness of it all. 'He couldn't utilize his business skills in case it brought him to anyone's attention as he wanted to stay under the radar and avoid any repercussions by the gutter pressœs'.

Blake was furious on her father's behalf, but also admired him greatly, he must be an extremely honourable man to put the love of his wife above the value of money, and he actually felt a little ashamed.

'They really loved each?' he mused allowed

'Oh yes, they still do' she smiled fondly 'They had to live very simply to enable them to save every penny they could but eventually they had enough to buy a rundown property and convert it into a modest hotel in Switzerland. He had to leave his own country to escape his father' she replied bitterly, then seemed to shake herself out of her morose thoughts. 'Of course using the English version of our surname helped to shield us' she smiled at him over her shoulder and watched his brow furrow in confusion.

'Filipo translates to Phillips in English' she said seeing his confusion. 'Me and rob were home schooled by our parents, they were concerned about our identities being discovered and putting us at risk' she sighed 'We had a good childhood all in all but very few friends apart from the occasional child that stayed at the hotel.

We were loved and brought up multi lingual, but later on in our teens we had allocution lessons to lose our accent, again helping us to keep hidden' she relaxed back into him.

She didn't want to go into any further details for the moment, she'd given him enough to satisfy his curiosity plus she did not want him to see how stupid and naïve she'd been. Or how hard they'd had to fight to have any kind of a 'normal life' she only added 'some people go to great lengths working an angle if they think they can profit from it' and shrugged.

He'd already been witness to her recent humiliation at Edmonton's hand, and that was just down to a man being fickle, nothing compared to the way she had been treated at the hands of another.

She finished by giving him a quick rundown of the various jobs she'd had from admin to interior design skipping over any rough patches. She also didn't explain anything about Rob's history apart from his knack for staff training and motivational speaking, for which he was in huge demand and paid well for his time. The rest was Rob's to tell not hers, anything else he wanted to know she'd tell him eventually.

She just needed some time to reassure herself that he wanted her for her and not for what she could mean to his business or fortune. She found it almost impossible to trust completely but with everything she'd been through, she'd learned the hard way that being cautious was a necessity.

'So, are you sorry you asked yet?' she asked trying to lighten the atmosphere and he could see the fear and vulnerability she hid behind false bravado and hugged her tightly against his chest.

'Not at all, thank you for sharing and your secret is safe with me' he added as he pulled back and kissed the tip of her nose. 'There is one thing I'd like to know though?' he ignored the fact that she'd stiffened against him '

What's your full name?' his breath whispering against her ear sent a frisson of awareness down her spine and she shivered in response. Then groaned leaning her forehead against his and huffed

'Kata, Carlotta, Corinne, Maria, Angelina, filipo' she said watching as his eyebrows rose

'Wow, that's quite a mouthful' he grinned 'Why, so many'? She linked her hands behind the back of his neck and looked at him steadily

'They originally wanted a large family but she had to have an emergency hysterectomy after our difficult birth' she said guiltily and shrugged 'I guess I got all the girls names she'd collected in one go, Rob just got dad's name but backwards' and grinned

'Guess her boy's list wasn't so long?' he said

'They called me Kitty for short well apart from when dad and rob want to torment me, then its kitten' she added wrinkling her nose. 'Kita actually means cat in Farsi/Persian' she said

'It suit's you' he said his eyes roaming over her face and he grinned wickedly as he bent her backwards over his arm and whispered huskily in her ear 'Those green eyes are very cat like and did you know you make this amazing purring sound when I' his words cut off abruptly as she pulled a hand from around his neck and slapped it over his mouth to stop him finishing. His eyes were full of laugher over her hand as she blushed from head to toe, he bit her palm playfully and she jerked it away scowling at him as he threw his head back and laughed. She punched him lightly in the chest and he sobered

'I think it's adorable that you can still blush after all the things we've done' he said waggling his eyebrows suggestively. She grew aroused as she felt him harden against her bottom and gasped in shock as he stood up and threw her over his shoulder.

'In fact it's given me a few ideas' he said laughingly as she squealed and swatted his behind 'I want to see what else makes you purr' he rubbed her naked behind and growled as he gave it a playful nip as he carried her giggling hysterically back through to the bedroom.

Much later on Kitty curled her sated body around his as he lay back against the pillows, one arm behind his head and listened contentedly to his heavy breathing. He deserved to rest for a while, he'd made good on his promise and had made her purr several times before allowing his own release. She'd never known that making love could be so overwhelming but it was and it had definitely been making love. She groaned into her pillow to hide the sound as she admitted to herself that she'd stupidly gone and done it. She was in deep trouble, she'd fell for him and the thought scared her stupid. It was going to destroy her when it was over, then she yawned tiredly and let the worry go, there was nothing she could do about it. She fell asleep tucked against him, warm and safe, for now!

Blake tried to rest, had pretended to sleep until he'd heard her breathing deepen eventually, after she'd shifted around for a while. He then lay still rubbing her shoulder, not sure if it was for her benefit or to comfort himself. He stared at the ceiling as he finally admitted that he had deeper feelings for her. He'd felt a connection to her that had always been missing with other women and as they'd made love and he admitted it was love he'd remembered the glimpse of something he'd had the other day and groaned quietly in distress.

He had noticed her, maybe from the beginning, subconsciously at least, because whether he liked it or not for the last year or more he remembered that is was always tilted green eyes he saw as his release hit. God he was such an idiot he thought as he banged his head back into his pillow. No wonder he'd not been able to look at her properly, he'd been afraid and ashamed at the same time.

He came to the unhappy conclusion that he'd lost interest in dating recently, well if that's what you could call it because he'd been riddled with guilt, subconsciously at least he knew he was using them as a substitute for the woman he was lusting after but was too stubborn to admit to. He lifted a handful of her hair and inhaled deeply, feeling peace washing over him as her now familiar scent wrapped around him. He was finally where he wanted to be, with the woman he needed to be with and nodded off. He held her securely against him with one arm around her and the other tangled in her hair, as if afraid she'd disappear while he slept.

They spent the rest of the day lounging around in his apartment, snacking on quick easy meals, which he loved watching her eat. She really enjoyed her food not like most of the women he'd dated but there again she had Italian blood running through her veins, so it shouldn't come as a surprise. They talked about anything and everything. He told her about his plans for the hotel as he lounged back against the sofa and she told him a little about the hotel her family owned in Switzerland.

'Maybe I'll get to see it one day?' he said as he ran his hand through her hair as she sat between his knees on the floor, he really hoped he would, he wanted to make a go of things with her because he instinctively knew she was the only one he had any kind of a chance at a fulfilled life with. He felt bone deep fear hit at the thought of losing her and made an effort to relax.

'I think you'd prefer the love nests' she'd said with a grin at him over her shoulder and he frowned 'Rob's idea, we have several log cabins dotted about the area that are specially tailored to lovers' she said 'we offer a special service in romance' and rolled her eyes at his shocked expression 'it's not what you think' she tutted 'I'll show you the website later' she said and put her head back against his knees, content to just be quiet for a while.

He sat back in the silence for now, he still didn't know everything he wanted to know about her but he knew enough for now and she seemed to be relaxing with him. Slowly letting down her guard and opening up, they still had time to learn about each other but he was not looking forward to taking her back to her flat later on. He liked having her around, he especially liked sleeping and waking with her in his arms.

Maybe he could talk her into letting him stay with her tonight he thought as he played with her hair, he found it rather soothing but they'd have to make a move soon. It was getting late and he had a busy week ahead of him. He was also worried that as soon as he left she'd find a way to put the walls back up.

Chapter Fourteen

Blake did stay over at Kitty's that night and he'd presumed that would be how they would progress, he was ready to settle down, to his complete shock. He wanted them to move in together, to give it a try and they had spent the first month together day and night at either his place or hers, he was truly happy and content with his lot for the first time in years.

They went out to restaurants, the cinema, walking in the park he'd even gone ice skating with her, then everything had changed.

He'd had a late business meeting out of town and as she'd looked so tired he'd said he didn't need her along, a lie of course. He'd always need her and god he'd missed her that night, hated not being able to turn over and feel her body next to his. That was when things changed, she changed, there was no longer every night together, she'd point blank refused to move in with him. She wanted to take a step back, slow things down, he needed to be patient, to give her time, but how much time did she need?

****

They'd been dating for 3 months now and it was Christmas in a few weeks, he'd secretly booked one of those romantic chalets her family had in Switzerland, Rob had been very accommodating. He'd told him he wanted to take her there to propose on New Year's Eve, she'd have her family near as well to help them celebrate. He'd been so sure it was the right thing to do, the only thing that would sort this mess out but now he was unsure of her response.

It was driving him insane not being able to touch her in work as she didn't want people to know about them. He was only allowed to stay at weekends and she only stayed with him on a Wednesday night. He was frustrated as hell and it was beginning to affect his work and concentration.

What the hell was going on? Did she even love him? He was shocked to realise that she'd never actually said the words, but there again neither had he, he'd just presumed she knew. He'd been so close at times though, especially as she slept curled around him after making love, those were the times they were close, really close, the only time he felt complete now. But then they'd arrive at work and that mask of professionalism would drop over her face and his happiness would shatter.
What was he, her dirty little secret?

He'd told his family all about them and they were hurt that he hadn't took her around, he'd tried when Mel had given birth to Lisa and Alice last month, but she'd refused saying it was too soon to meet his family, how long did she want? He didn't know how much longer he could live this double life, happy with her, but miserable at the same time, it was torture.

Kitty was utterly miserable she loved Blake so much but didn't know if she could trust him? She'd started to receive photo's a month after the gallery showing. The first had arrived while he'd been away on business, he'd not taken her with him, saying she'd looked tired. They were always anonymous, coming through the internal mail at work. They were intimate pictures, not naked ones, they were much worse. In the first one, their heads were together talking privately, his hand covering the back of her head, no details of his companion visible.

Or else it would be one of Blake facing the camera, looking at someone, a woman of course, you could tell because he'd have a look of absolute longing on his face. They were the worse ones, she couldn't make out who the woman was on any of them, the details were always fuzzy as if altered to hide her identity but the ook on his face would haunt her for days. She couldn't sleep after she received those ones. She'd refuse his offer of company that night just wanting to wallow in her absolute misery, to lick her wounds in private.

He was pulling away from her, she could feel it, he was getting frustrated she could sense it. She just didn't know what to do about it because she didn't know if it was because he wanted out and didn't want to upset her, therefore lose a P A. Or if it was because he was just as miserable as she was with their relationship, and this had all been a huge misstate, or was he unhappy with the total lack of commitment, because he loved her. That's the one she wanted it to be. But how could she commit to a man if she was unsure if he could be faithful.

She was afraid to go out in public with him anymore, in case they were photographed. What if he was seeing someone else and this woman saw the pictures and confronted her? She'd know for sure then and she really didn't want to lose him. This was no good, she wasn't helping herself. She needed to do something to distract herself, take her mind off the whole sorry mess.

Lance had been a complete pain in the arse, trying to fight the sale of the Bellville. That was the little matter Blake had been trying to sort out on the Sunday after the gallery showing. He'd thrown all sorts of spanners in the works, it was illegal, it was immoral, he had the right to take the business, all ludicrous and Blake's stepfather had been working behind the scenes trying to sort out the problems with staffing and orders that had continued to be messed up.

Poor Jake was beside himself with worry thinking he was back to losing everything but suddenly Lance had just backed down and given up. It had been a long fight but they were all meeting at the hotel tomorrow morning to finalise the paperwork. She was driving up with Blake, and Len and Mike were meeting them there to finalise everything and get the ball rolling on the renovations.

Blake had also said he had a surprise for her and she'd find out what it was when they got there. Another sleepless night for her then, she would now spend the night worrying over what it was, the visions were horrendous. "Oh hey Kitty meet my new lover, I don't need you around now so I replaced you after I got fed up, you were no longer a challenge" she shuddered at the picture show playing in her head..

She had refused to meet his family although she would have loved it, she was desperate to hold those sweet babies, Alice and Lisa. She was scared though, what if it was true and they knew about it? How awful would it be sitting with people that were feeling sorry for you, she needed to get a grip, her paranoia was getting the better of her, and she'd never sleep at this rate? She punched her pillow and Blake's scent was released, he'd slept there last night, she hadn't changed the sheets, she needed the comfort of his familiar smell. "You're pathetic" she told herself as the first tears began to fall, was he with her now? Was he making love to her? She scrubbed her hand over her eyes to remove the pesky tears. Why did she always seem to be crying? She was going to have to go see a doctor soon. Her scanty periods had disappeared, maybe her ovary had packed in altogether? Her hormones were wreaking havoc, which would certainly explain her moods. Or maybe it was due to her being stressed out and miserable, it wouldn't be the first time it had happened, they usually disappeared when she was overwrought.

Blake had a restless night, he needed Kitty. He was kidding himself if he thought he could let her go, she had become as necessary to him as air. He hoped she liked her surprise and that it broke the holding pattern that they'd been in. He needed a miracle to win her around and he was hoping that this would finally turn the tide in his favour. The only problem was he wasn't going to be fit to get through the day if he didn't get some sleep, he looked at the clock 12pm and cursed, who was he kidding. He pulled a coat on over a pair of jogging bottoms, slipped his feet in his shoes, grabbed a suit bag and some fresh underwear and made his way to his car in the underground car park. He'd be damned if he was going to spend another night tossing and turning.

Kitty was lay in the dark thinking, nothing unusual about that apart from her heart started to bang so loudly she could hear it. Then she turned her head and caught the shadow at her French window and froze, her heart really did start up a rapid tattoo now. Her mouth dried and she nearly fell on the floor in shock when the shadow moved and she heard knocking on the French door, not her heart then. Whoever it was they obviously weren't here to rob her, she thought and rolled her eyes as they banged again. She slipped out of bed and opened the blinds and there stood Blake, huddled into his coat with a suit bag thrown over his shoulder.

'Come on Kitten open up its bloody freezing' he said from the other side of the glass, her hungry eyes roamed over his body taking in his tired eyes. Hi hair mussed up, as if he'd spent hours running his hands through it, in frustration, or she thought cynically, maybe someone else had been running their hands through it? 'Please, I know I shouldn't be here but I just want to hold you, please' he begged again, and her heart actually turned over in her chest, he sounded as miserable as her. She turned the key and pulled the left side of the door open and he slipped through. She locked it and shut the blinds again and turned, he was already stripping out of his clothes. His suit bag hung over the chair and his coat thrown on top of it. Standing in only his briefs he grabbed her hand and tugged her over to the bed and pulled her down beside him. He wrapped his arm around her waist and spooned in behind her and then sighed as he nuzzled her hair and kissed her neck.

'Thank you' he said then yawned and that quickly his breathing grew heavy as one of his legs slid between hers and he fell asleep. She linked her fingers with his over her stomach and her eyes drifted closed as she joined him, her exhausted mind finally settling. Her last thought was of how much easier it was to sleep when he was there.

Chapter Fifteen

'Bollocks!' she heard Blake say as he started to strip off his briefs and quickly stepped into fresh ones, she rolled over and looked at the time, her eyes widening in alarm.

'It's 8am' she sputtered as she dove out of bed and started to strip out of her night shirt, a green one that Blake had bought for her. She hopped from foot to foot as she stepped into clean panties.

'Damn' he said and she looked over her shoulder at him about to question him when she spotted his eyes on her bare breasts. She tutted in annoyance and heard his laughter, then it muffled as he tugged a shirt over his head and she continued dressing.

'Promise me you'll jiggle about like that one morning, when we're not rushing' he said as he kissed her head as she struggled to fasten a pair of trousers, one of the new ones she'd bought for the office, they were fitted, showing off her curves but seemed a trifle snug around the waist at the moment. He'd complained so much about her "work sacks", that was what he'd started to call her work clothes, and as he was already aware of who she was and who her parents were, she no longer needed to try and disguise herself. She'd thrown them out and replaced them with more modern ones. She'd just finished brushing mascara onto her lashes and tying her hair back in a loose ponytail as he'd come back into the bedroom with 2 coffee's to go.

'Ready Kitten?' he asked, his eyes sweeping over her appreciatively, as she put her make up bag back in the dresser drawer. He was always hungry for her but he'd become scared of being intimate with her recently, scared he'd slip up and say something in the heat of passion that couldn't be taken back. It was like walking on egg shells with her, the only real time she was affectionate now was in bed and even that had its limits. He sighed in resignation, something had to give and soon he thought, he was ready to explode but was terrified of her walking away, a definite first for him. It was driving him crazy.

She took the cup off him with a smile and led the way out. The tension was back between them, it was thick in the car but neither of them seemed to know how to break through it! She'd been surprised when he'd just turned up out of the blue and even more shocked when all he wanted to do was cuddle up to her and sleep, what was going on?

Was that the actions of a guilty man or one of a man just mixed up with what was going on?

She really wished she had the answer. She could ask of course, but did she really want to know if it was going to rip out her heart?

They nipped into the office, Kitty to check that she hadn't missed moving any appointments and Blake to pick up some paperwork to take with him, Audrey was due in shortly.

She sat down at her desk, as he disappeared through his door. Her hand froze her heart beating painfully in her chest and her breath freezing in her lungs. There tucked under her keypad was an envelope, a cream one, exactly like all the other ones she'd received. Her hands shook as she opened it, making sure Blake was still in his office. She closed her eyes and took a deep breath before pulling the picture out. Did she really want to see this one? This could be the one that put an end to all her fantasies about happy ever after and she felt her heart crack a little.

She took another breath and blew it out slowly as she opened her eyes and looked down at it, her breath hitching as she held back a sob. His head was back in laughter in this one his eyes alight with joy as he looked to the side at someone just out of shot. She was so engrossed in looking at it that she didn't hear him come up behind her.

'That was when we were at the park' Blake said taking the picture from her, 'how on earth did you manage to take it when you were sat with me?' he sounded genuinely puzzled. Then his words registered

'What do you mean, it's of us?' she asked frowning up at him and he looked down into her watery eyes. His heart lodged in his throat, all the pieces clicking into place, how could he have been so blind?

'Oh god Kitten, you think I've been seeing someone else?' he said sounding stricken, his eyes taking on a haunted quality as she just nodded, her face pale as she stared at the picture, then she reached into the bottom drawer of her desk and pulled out a dozen more envelopes, each contained one picture only. They were all labelled for Kitty's attention, and not one contained a letter or explanation.

He did notice that every single one of them was of times when they'd been alone, eating at a fast food joint, walking hand in hand in the park, outside the cinema's, coming out of a room at the Bellville and a few more. He remembered every single one?
Every smile, every touch, how could she not remember?
Did it mean so little to her?
Did he mean so little to her?
He'd locked away the memories of the good times they'd shared, the laughter the fun, how could she have forgotten? His stomach knotted with tension, annoyance at being unjustly accused of something, his temper ratcheting up until he took a closer look at each one. Unbelievable, he was the only person visible in each shot, Kitty's face or whole body made fuzzy and unrecognisable,

and the background scenes had been altered. He ground his teeth in anger, not at Kitty but at whoever had set out to hurt her intentionally and cause a rift in their relationship.

She was afraid to speak, afraid he was going to break her heart here and now, shatter her into a thousand pieces like humpty dumpty and she'd never be whole again.

Blake was staggered, how on earth could she possibly think he'd been cheating on her? How? Why? The questions began running in circles through his head, then he looked down at her shaking hands and noticed the cream envelope she was holding in a death grip. He pulled it from her nerveless fingers and turned it over in his hands. It was one of the company envelopes, the DP symbol on the back, for Dennison properties and he crumpled it up in his fist. He pulled her up from her chair and crushed her against his chest.

'I would never cheat on you, you of all people are safe from that, I'm sorry honey I should have told you how much I love you' he heard her gasp and her fingers dug into his back as she rubbed her face on his chest.

He pulled back to look down at her, her eyes were wet, tear drops suspended from her lashes, and his heart missed a beat.

'You never said, I didn't know' she said on a hiccup 'god I love you too Blake so much but this has been killing me' she admitted as she buried her face in his chest again, his arms like bands of steel around her. He buried his face in her hair and inhaled her familiar and much needed scent and for the first time in weeks, the constriction began easing around his chest making it easier to take a proper breath again. She loved him too, they could sort this mess out, how could he have been so blind to her pain, this was what all the pulling away had been about, she really thought he was just playing with her.

It was a little earlier than he intended and not in the romantic setting of the wooden chalet he'd envisioned, where they would be cuddled together in front of a roaring open fire. Virgin snow surrounding the building and tumbling passed the windows, but now was definitely the time. He moved back and grabbed her hand dragging her across to his office and closing the door behind them. He had a sense of déjà vu as he turned to face her.

This was the very place it had all started, locked in his office, her standing looking at him like a bunny caught in headlights, and he suddenly smiled.

Maybe this was the right place, as he moved behind his desk and pulled open his top drawer and removed the small velvet box he'd had nestled there for the last 6 weeks.

Kitty bit her lip in anxiety, he'd told her he loved her, he'd also asked if she thought he'd been cheating, but he'd not actually denied it. There again he'd said the photo was one of them out together, she was confused, what the hell was going on and why was the room suddenly spinning? Her vision wavering at the edges. The floor was getting closer and closer to her and she couldn't figure out what was happening and then everything went black as she felt herself falling.

Blake heard Kitty gasp behind him and turned in time to see her swaying, her face drained completely of colour and he just managed to catch her before she hit the floor.

He sat on the sofa with her on his lap, her breathing shallow and her body limp, what the hell had just happened, why had she fainted?. He heard the lift doors open in the outer office and called out.

'What on earth is the matter?

Why are you shouting?' Audrey asked as she pushed through his door and gasped as she spotted Kitty lay limp across his lap, her eyes closed and her face deathly pale.

'Call an ambulance please' he said, he felt her pulse and let out a relieved breath, it was a little slow but strong. Audrey ran to the phone on his desk and dialled 999 and requested an ambulance giving Kitty's details and answering the questions about whether she was conscious and breathing.

Kitty had just started to come around as the ambulance crew arrived, she put up a fuss, but Blake wasn't having any of it, she'd scared 10 years off his life, he wanted her checked out at the hospital. She gave in, too weak to protest at the moment, her head was banging and she felt sick, her stomach rolling as they strapped her onto a trolley. She felt foolish as the lift door opened up in the lobby and people looked towards them, then she spotted a woman coming through the door and her eyes opened wide.

'What's wrong?' Blake asked at her side looking around to see what could have caused the shocked look on her face.

'Why is Lance's Assistant here?' she asked and Blake's head shot around 'where, which one?' she pointed to a slender brunette that was heading towards the stairs and he gave security the nod to stop and question her.

'I'll have them ring my mobile once they have answers' he told her as they moved towards the ambulance, but he had his suspicions, ones he wasn't willing to share just yet but he would once he made sure that she was okay after being checked over.

'You can't come with me!' she said as he went to get in the back of the ambulance

'I most certainly can and will' he said and sat down on the chair provided as the paramedic checked her heart rate, blood pressure and pulse.

'Blake you need to get to the hotel' she said exasperated with him and he just snorted

'Not until I know what's going on with you I don't' his face a mask of stubbornness, his square chin set as he ground his teeth in annoyance. He pulled out his mobile and hit redial on the buttons, and spoke quietly into it once it was answered, trying not to disturb her as she answered the paramedic's questions. He put his phone away and looked at her, she'd just been asked about her monthly cycle

'She hasn't had one in the 3 months we've been together, no she's not on contraception, yes we use a condom but she also only has one ovary and it doesn't function as it should' he told the paramedic, watching Kitty's mouth open and close and the young man just shook his head and grinned as he wrote all the information down on his report.

'What?' he asked as she still stared at him 'do you really think I'm not aware of what your bodies doing?' he snorted 'please, give me some credit, I'm always aware of your body' he said with a grimace 'trust me' and she smiled brightly at him for the first in what seemed like weeks.

1 hour later in the hospital Blake and Kitty watched the monitor as the wand swept over her stomach

'Yep I'm sure you're pregnant' the stenographer said 'See there's the head, the belly, the spine, the legs and that noise in the back ground, that whooshing sound, is a very healthy heartbeat' he looked back at their stunned faces 'congratulations, you are about 14 weeks pregnant by my measurements, sometimes it's good when science is proven wrong' he winked and looked towards the doctor.

Kitty was too stunned to say anything, was that really her baby on the screen, and what on earth was Blake going to think? They hadn't discussed having a family, she hadn't thought it was worth bringing up. I mean she'd told him the first and only time they'd had unprotected sex that she couldn't have them and gasped, her eyes searching for his.

Blake was in love, his child, he was looking at his child, growing in Kitty's womb and he felt like he was going to explode with happiness.

He looked over at her and noticed she was watching him anxiously and then looking towards the screen again.

`

'Are you not happy about it?' he asked quietly and held his breath while he waited for her to reply. Her eyes met his briefly before slipping away.

'Yes of course I am, it's just come as a shock that's all, and oh god Blake I'm so sorry' she rushed on. "I really didn't think this would happen' she added as her eyes filled with tears. He got off his chair and scooted onto the bed at the side of her and wrapped his arms around her. The stenographer and doctor moved discreetly away giving them some space.

'Do you remember what you told me after we made love the first time?' and she nodded rubbing her cheek against his chest 'Well I guess we got our miracle' he said and kissed her mouth then pulled the box out of his jacket pocket and placed it in her hand. 'I was going to do this on New year's, booked a really romantic place in Switzerland I'd heard about and everything' he told her and watched her eyes widen 'then I decided that I couldn't wait that long and that's why I was dragging you into my office' he admitted 'You kind of cramped my style though, you could have waited to swoon until after I'd proposed' he mock pouted, then grinned at her shocked face and heard the doc and stenographer cough as if covering laughs. He smiled 'So kitten, I love you more than life itself, will you marry me?' he said solemnly and watched as her eyes filled with tears 'You really should, you know' he added 'I mean what will our families think, you'll have to make an honest man of me' he said grinning at the picture still emblazoned on the screen of their growing child and leaned down and kissed her still flat stomach. 'I don't know why you're so shocked, didn't you once say that I excel at everything I put my mind to' and the whole room lit up with laughter as she scowled at him but couldn't hold onto it, her happiness showing in her glowing cheeks and sparkling eyes.

She was ready to burst with joy, she was getting everything she'd ever wished for but didn't think she'd get. Her guardian angel seemed to have been putting in some overtime. She couldn't speak, her throat constricted with tears of happiness but her eyes shone with love as she nodded. He swooped in and fused his mouth with hers, alleviating any need to answer, then slipped an exquisite but tasteful diamond and emerald ring on her finger and kissed that too.

'Congratulations, would you like a picture for prosperity?' the stenographer asked and they both nodded.

Kitty still had hold of the baby scan picture as they got into the taxi that was taking them to the airport. They were on their way to Switzerland for a break, time to be alone and relax away from all the stress that had surrounded them over the last several months.

Chapter Sixteen

They'd arrived at the Bellville, 5 days later in time for a celebratory meal Blake was now sole owner and her surprise had been that he'd talked her father and brother into coming over to get it up and running for him. She had wandered where he was while they were in Switzerland. Her mother had been there of course and was charmed by Blake, she'd also been ecstatic at the news that she was going to be a grandmother. Antonio was going to get the hotel in shape and Rob was going to get the staff's training up to scratch. She'd been shocked but happy to see them and after her father had been assured that his daughter was well and blissfully happy he'd welcomed Blake to the family.

Lance, had turned out to be behind it all, from the photo's to the hotel's problems. He'd put people on his payroll and then placed them in strategic places to cause maximum damage without closing the hotel.

He'd been at University with Blake, he was from old money and had taken an instant dislike to him because he'd worked his way up on sheer bloody mindedness and talent. He'd wanted to take him down a peg or two and show him that the working class had no right to play in the upper echelons world of power and money.

He'd gone after kitty to hurt him emotionally because he'd seen the way Blake had looked at her. Then when he'd failed to hold on to her, he'd set out to destroy their happiness with doctored photographs taken by a sleazy photographer he'd hired. When they'd caught up with the photographer, he had provided them with the original prints; which showed Blake and Kitty together and blissfully happy. He'd also handed over taped conversations he'd had with Lance making requests for what he wanted and where.

He'd then sent his lover and temp assistant to an agency and made sure she was employed by Dennison Developments so she was on hand to deliver the doctored pictures.

They would probably have been still trying to prove it all if not for Blake's step father Greg; he'd been invaluable with his connections in law and personal security.

Dear old Lance was now on the run, as the police were looking for him to help with their enquiries in conjunction with several different business related frauds and extortion. They didn't expect to see him again, he'd probably crawl back out of hiding, once he thought he was safe. That was never going to happen, Blake had already set the ball in motion, and he'd offered a reward for anyone with information relating to his present whereabouts.

Kitty had also come clean about her disastrous first engagement and how it had been the final straw for her leaving everything behind and her finding employment with him. He wasn't happy about the way she'd been treated but he would always be eternally grateful that she'd ended up with him.

Epilogue

They'd been married 6 months now, they'd had a quiet ceremony attended by family and a few close friends. Kitty had been radiant and beautiful in a simply cut ivory dress as she'd walked to him on her father's arm. Blake was very fond of his in-laws, his mother in law was a tiny older blonde version of his wife, she had a quiet strength about her, didn't rile but had this amazing way of fluttering her lashes and he husband would jump to do her bidding. It still amazed him immensely to see the large still mostly black haired, handsome Italian jump to please his wife, she really did have him wrapped around her finger. It was wonderful to watch them together, they still held hands and disappeared for time alone together after over 30 years of marriage. It gave him hope for their own.

Blake's musings ended as he lifted his sleeping son out of the arms of his wife; he still got a kick out of saying that, she'd dozed off while breast feeding him.

He placed him against his shoulder and gently rubbed his back to get rid of any wind he'd swallowed with his milk. He kissed his soft cheek and rubbed his cheek against his soft wispy black hair enjoying this quiet time with his little family. Once he was satisfied he'd settled, he put him carefully into his large rocking crib at the bottom of the bed and covered him up, tucking the edges in so he couldn't move.

He moved back around the bed and slipped in beside Kitty, careful not to disturb her as he wrapped his arm around her and rested it on her now flat stomach. He'd not been able to curl up with her for the last 5 days, since Blaine's birth. He'd arrived 2 weeks early on the grand opening night of the New Bellville hotel and put him into a total panic. 18 hours of hell, he'd torturously watched her endure before they'd finally had to use forceps to pull his screaming 6lb 8oz, tiny, beautiful son into the world. A few hours later and a major scare due to her haemorrhaging because her placenta didn't dislodge properly; until they gave it a little help and he'd finally been able to breathe again. She hadn't needed a transfusion but had needed a little more time to recover.

'Welcome home' he whispered as she turned over and curled into his chest, resting her hand on his stomach. He smiled into the darkness. He'd missed feeling her curled against him as she slept, she'd never gotten over the habit of drawing circles on his stomach as she drifted off, and he'd found himself unable to sleep without it.

He'd spent the last few days dozing in a recliner in the corner of her private hospital room, refusing to leave until his family did.

His world was once again as it should be, his wife and son were home and his new hotel was flourishing, thanks the wonderful refurbishment work that had been done. Kitty had designed each room herself, down to colours, material and furniture. Now all he had to do was figure out what was going on with his brother-in-law, Rob. He was definitely up to something as he was still hanging around.

****

God it was good to be home and in her own bed, in the new house her and Blake had chosen and decorated together, it had been a busy couple of months, she conceded.
Kitty was tired but elated after the last few days, but it was wonderful to be able to cuddle up to her "husband" wow, she wasn't sure that would ever get old. She had a fabulous husband,

she smiled to herself as she felt sleep claim her, a beautiful little boy and all was right with her world. She frowned, no not quite right. Her sneaky brother was up to something? She intended to get to the bottom of it, now she was back on her feet. Her last thought was it had to do with a woman, as she finally succumbed to a much needed sleep.

About the author

J F Holland is a stay at home mum with 6 children and a menagerie of animals. She still lives in the small town, in Manchester UK, where she was born and attended school. She's always had a love of romance books and spent a lot of time as a child re-writing the fairy stories she read.

She can be contacted through her Facebook page at :-

www.facebook.com/pages/J-F-Holland-Romance-Writer

Or

You can e-mail her at:- jfholland_author@aol.co.uk

Message from the Author:-

This is my debut book 'The Only One' and I hope you enjoyed reading Blake and Kitty's story, as much as I enjoyed writing it. If you'd like to read more in the Dennison Property Stories.

Rob's Story 'This Time' is due out at the end of October 2015

Feedback is always welcome.

45823840R00137

Made in the USA
Charleston, SC
04 September 2015